THE LAST CYCLE

THE SKYWARD SAGA

BOOK 6

A.R. KNIGHT

1 / AWAKE

Do you know the dreams you have when you think you're dreaming forever? They're slow at first, an endless series of stories, each one less and less real as you begin to find the flaws.

Flashes of leafy canopies, my bright-lit home mingle with the fantastic. I share dinners with Father and Mother. Hunts with Malo and Viera through dense jungle and damp caves. Even T'Oli, the creamy Ooblot joins me as we climb through the sewers of a now-dead planet.

I know none of this is real.

Because I'm supposed to be dead.

And yet.

I'm not me anymore: the way you become intimate with your body over time, one season after another of touching your muscles and moving, jumping, thinking. Those connections are gone. I am adrift in an unfamiliar sea of strands. I cast out, trying to find parts of myself.

Answers come slow. Tentative. Like a flowers blooming after the first rains, each connection is beautiful. Fragile.

A voice from everywhere, nowhere tells me they will get stronger with time.

The voice echoes in my dreams. Changes, too. Sometimes its Malo saying the words, veering away from our hunt to offer an explanation of why I can't speak, or see yet, even though I'm right there with him in the forest.

Other times, the voice fills a void of nothing. I'm between selves, a break in the stories and words of comfort come. The sounds of friends whispering to me wishes, compassion. Things I hold on to in the dark.

Nerves had to be repaired, the voice tells me as I wander through the ash wastes of Earth's far side. New strands grown and connected. Organs made using what limited examples exist of human biology. I don't know what it's talking about, but I hold on to the last thing the voice says: I am still a human.

When I see for the first time, a phantom centers my eyes. My friend. One who, last I checked, was barely conscious. Had just been loosed from the clutches of a creature so evil that it took the very freedom away from Malo's soul. But there he is, in front of me, his head wearing short black hair, still gaunt but smiling anyway. His shoulders show the long arc of ash-inked tattoos across his chest and arms as he leans over me. As he brushes my forehead.

"Empress," Malo says and his voice is slow, soft, as if I'm made of glass that might shatter should he talk too loud. "Welcome back."

The welcome comes with a barrage. I'm greeted first by Malo and then a parade of others, most straight from my dreams. A healthy Viera, though she still sports a bandage around her head. Lan, the emerald-scaled Oratus who keeps her four claws clasped and head bowed, who offers her thanks in a low hiss. Lastly, with Malo still by my side, comes the huge bulk of Kolas, commander of the Vincere force dedicated to the extermination of the galaxy's enemies.

With each of them comes bits and pieces of the story that brought me from the end of the Sevora War to a long and wide red sponge bed on Kolas' cruiser, the *Nunilite*.

Malo and T'Oli had made the docking bay on the seed ship.

Ignos, the Sevora that had at one point been inside me and that had, back on the seed ship, been so determined to return to its place of power, had left the shuttle we arrived in undefended. T'Oli and Malo took the craft, lifted off, and made the leap back to Vimelia, the Sevora home world where Kolas and his fleet were still cleaning up the remnants of their enemy.

Kolas came back with them, and a seed ship left empty by Viera and my efforts presented little trouble. Eventually, a Vincere strike team cut into the center and found me.

"You were dead," Malo says.

"Actually," slaps T'Oli, who's oozed its way up Malo's side and rests on his shoulders, both eyestalks bobbing at me. "She was in the state called a coma. A living paralysis. Not really dead, but not really alive. Catastrophic failure of several organs. She would have died, though—"

"She gets it," Malo says to the blob, then looks back at me. "We put you back together."

I try to ask what that means? Only my voice doesn't work. Not yet, anyway. But my hands do, and when they get the message, I write out the words. The questions.

It turns out there's an advantage to being a species grown by experimentation. An advantage to being designed by another. Kolas has an Amigga with his fleet. One who is able to pull up the secret records of humanity's existence. One able to find out how I function, and with that information put me back together. The Amigga wove new organs, new nerves and cells from vats of biological material and built me back. As I hear all of this, I can only think of what Ignos told me when it first crashed through the sky and took up residence in my mind: *I will bring you miracles.*

"Kolas says we'll be leaping soon to the Chorus," Malo says some time later—I'm drifting in and out of consciousness, and as T'Oli puts it, time has little real meaning in space. There are no days, no seasons, only Cycles; major events marking the passing of eras. Despite that unsettling description, I know Malo has barely left my side. Only when I order him to sleep does he leave. "Apparently they want you to be the emissary for humanity," Malo flashes me a smile. "I can't think of anyone better."

"I don't want to," I manage to say—my voice is coming back in spurts, what I'm told is the result of new muscles. Ones that need to grow and train. I won't be able to run far for a while either, or breathe too heavy, or eat too much. All the result of organs learning their place in a new body.

"I don't think you have a choice." There's real sadness in Malo's eyes. "I wish you did. I wish we could just go home. But Kolas says we're needed now."

"Why?"

"Apparently we need to prove the Chorus we can be trusted. We need to stand up and proclaim our allegiance to them."

"Why? I know I just asked, but what does the Chorus need from us?"

Malo shakes his head. "Kolas would not tell me. He only said, since you owe the Chorus your life, you must do this."

I close my eyes for a moment. The last time I owed an Amigga a favor, the last time I had to do what an Amigga said, it nearly ripped me apart. Dalachite, on another space station an eternity ago, threatened to use me as a project for its own research. Getting involved with the Amigga is a quick way to die, or worse. Why would I help them now? My life or no?

"Kolas also told me," Malo continues and now his voice is even sadder, as if not only what he's saying is tragic, but ugly and distasteful. Exposing a weakness in himself. "They'll destroy Earth, Kaishi. If we don't give the Chorus what they want, they'll send the Vincere to complete what they tried before."

That's more like the Amigga I know. Pose generous, and seal the deal with a threat.

Well, I've seen worse.

As if waiting for Malo to complete setting the stage for my new life, the door to my room swishes open to reveal someone new. The

Amigga. Unlike Dalachite, the one that ran *Cobalt*, or Sapphrite, the leader of Clarity's Dawn and the resistance beneath the surface of Vimelia, this one is different. This one is smaller, a healthy gray-blue color that does nothing to stop the queasy shifting of my stomach as I look at a ball without eyes, without arms. It's encased in a translucent sheath, one with the barest hint of yellow on the fringes. The Amigga floats on a set of micro-jets around the base and sides. No mechanical arms, but strange, pocked circles are evenly spaced along a stripe around the Amigga's suit.

"Interfaces," the Amigga says as it notices me looking, as it floats into the room. "Bring me near a device, and I can interact. Form a connection and control. Useful on ships, when the more crude methods of metal arms and legs have less value."

I blink at the Amigga from my sponge bed, and notice Malo sitting rigid. Neither of us like Amigga. Neither of us enjoy the thing's presence, but I swallow my distaste. I put the crown on—not a real one, of course, but the one I have to wear at all times whether or not I'm in my palace or among my people. As Malo and Viera have told me; *Empress* is not a title to be worn at will, but rather bonded and lived with forever.

"I'm told you saved me," I say. My voice is getting stronger now. It has the volume, if not the flavor, of how I used to sound. "Thank you."

The Amigga hovers closer and Malo tenses, as if he's going to get up and punch the thing. I want to reach out and touch him, tell Malo no, don't worry. I don't think the Amigga is here to kill me. I don't even know if it could.

"I was glad to do so. Partly because no Amigga has helped a human before, and new intelligent species are so rare. A scientific first, which my name will forever be associated with." It's hard to know where to look when the Amigga speaks. There's no eyes, no mouth to focus on. The words come from the thing's suit, from speakers that cause the speech to reverberate through the small room. "My name is Ferrolite. I am the lead Amigga assigned to this fleet. It is my job to ensure that Kolas and his forces carry out the Chorus' demands. It is also my job to make sure I preserve those things of interest to the galaxy. Like you."

"Now you want something in return."

The Amigga has no capacity, that I can tell, to show surprise, shock, or disappointment. There's no emotions to read and since its voice comes through a mechanical synthesizer, it lacks the emotional tones a human might be able to put in. As such, with Ferrolite hovering before me, I have no idea whether the Amigga is happy or sad that I move immediately to business. But I'm tired, and if someone is going to ask something of me I'd rather know and be done with it.

"Human, Kaishi, the galaxy runs on a stable framework of species working beneath the Chorus to live fruitful, happy lives. We would welcome humanity within our community. But every species needs an ambassador, every species needs someone to bring it to the galactic stage. After what you've done I can think of no better."

"Because I destroyed a Sevora ship?"

"Because you demonstrated the things civilization values," Ferrolite says. "You are brave, courageous, intelligent and kind. Lan told me how you tried to rescue her and her pair, rather than escape and save yourself. Kolas told me how you gave everything to retrieve this one here on the Vimelia. These are laudable traits. These are valued. The Chorus is always looking to improve the make-up of the galaxy and if humanity is a reflection of you, then your species would be well appreciated."

It's hard not to like the Amigga's words. Hard not to feel a slight blush of pride, of embarrassment at being so singled out for something I thought was only the right thing to do. Yet, here I am, ready for more. I think it's because, having gone so long, across so many places, there hasn't been any outward acknowledgment of what we've done. My struggles have been made apart from the world I love, mostly apart from my species. Finally, here, as I claw my way back from death, I'm recognized.

"Will you?" Ferrolite gets to the question. "Will you add humanity's voice to the Chorus?"

I don't like the Amigga, I don't trust Ferrolite, but I can understand its motivations. I can sympathize with its goals; the Sevora are gone, the galaxy is on the brink of peace and prosperity. Any Empress would want to bring her people into that oasis. I have to think of everyone, not just myself.

"I will serve," I say. "Humanity will join your galaxy."

If there's any congratulations to be had for promising humanity's part will be played, Ferrolite doesn't give any. No fanfare bursts through the speakers, drinks and feasts don't appear. The Amigga only gives the briefest sound of approval, then floats away as if the only thing I'd agreed to is a moment's peace.

"You trust that thing?" Malo says.

"I don't have a choice, do I?" I reply. "Ferrolite put me back together. Without it, I wouldn't be here."

"That was its choice, this is yours."

"Then what should I say, Malo?" I look at my warrior, propped up in my bed. "What should I tell Avril, or all the refugees of Damantum when the Chorus declares them a threat and now, instead of scared Sevora, we're facing an Oratus army descending on Earth?"

Malo leans back against the side of the room. Stares across at the nothing on the far wall. "I just found freedom. I don't want to lose it again. Not yet."

"We won't," I say, though I don't know for sure. Another promise pledged in the dark. "I'll make them respect us."

Malo laughs, and the hollow bark cuts me. "Kaishi, we were pawns to the Sevora, and we're no different now. The Chorus doesn't need to respect us, because we aren't a threat, and we have nothing to offer them."

"That's not true. They made us, remember? An Amigga built us, created us because they wanted something better. The Chorus knows we're valuable."

Those words mollify Malo a little bit; he offers a half-hearted nod. Then his eyes go down to the tattoos on his chest. "All of these are lies, you know."

"Lies?"

"Ignos didn't create us. The Amigga did. All the gods, all of our society is based on lies."

"Now you're being sad." I fight back. "You don't know whether our Ignos had a hand in our creation or not, and even if the gods didn't directly control anything, the idea of them helped us survive. Helped our people grow, love, and learn."

"And when the Chorus arrives and starts telling every human they're a product of the Amigga? Like the crops we grow in our fields?"

That's a harder question to answer. I don't know how my own people would take that, the Ignos-worshiping Charre. Avril and her hardy, logical Lunare beneath the mountains might absorb the discovery in stride, but the society I lived in . . . would it stand up to such a revelation?

"It's still a secret, right?" I say. "We don't need to tell anyone. There's no point in it."

"The Chorus will."

"Not all of them know," I reply. "I don't think Ferrolite knows—it said we're a new species."

"Then we keep this a secret, for now?"

"When the Chorus comes to Earth, there'll be enough changes. I don't think we need to doubt our gods at the same time," I say, wanting as much to keep a hold of the rituals, the sayings and the beliefs I've held since my beginning as to keep my people from falling apart.

We keep at it, discussing, playing with our past as though it's something to be chosen or tossed aside depending on our whims. Until my own body catches up with me and I start missing words, start closing my eyes, and Malo does the nice thing and lets me claim victory by falling into a deep, deep sleep.

2 / THE PRISONER

Four of them, a true set and a terror to the Chorus' worst enemies. Sent across the galaxy on more missions than Sax can remember, each one a dizzying array of objectives, attacks, and merciless slaughters of species who dared defy the command of the galaxy's rulers. Each and every one of those missions plays, dragging Sax through a life lived at the fringe of sanity for far longer than he had any right to expect.

Starships crash, miners misfire, or an ambush catches a pair off-guard. There's a million ways an Oratus can die in this galaxy, and most of them don't live all that long for it. Yet Sax has seen enough to learn his way of life is wrong. Or, at least, it's in the service of the wrong thing. The wrong species.

Being alone with his thoughts is the worst thing Sax can imagine. Well, not the *worst* thing, because where he's at now, sequestered in a holding-tank of a cell, with a white ring-light up top for company, undercuts the awfulness of his imagination with the slicing knife of solitude. Not that Sax minds being alone—he prefers it to most company—but these tight walls, forming up square around the large Oratus, compress his single self until Sax is overcome with the impossible urge to

GET OUT.

The hissing roar goes nowhere. Bounces around the cage, makes Sax sick of his own voice. Still, it feels good to yell, to do something. He sticks out his foreclaw, running it along the chromed sides of his cell. There's not enough room for Sax to extend his arm fully, so the strike, when he makes it, is haphazard and awkward. Even so, an Oratus' strength should be enough to make a mark.

The walls remain unblemished. They show Sax's distorted reflection haloed in the light from above. Four arms sporting clawed hands, though his razors are no longer the organic originals. His claws gleam like the walls, like patches of his gray scales, ones stripped away and replaced with metal plating. Surgeries hiding the scars of his near death and giving evidence to the same. Sax's tail wraps around his squatting talons, its tip twitching on occasion as an outlet for fraying, frustrated nerves.

You gave yourself up for them.

That's the thought that keeps coming back. It calms Sax down, opens a mental gate to his pair and what Bas might be doing. Sax isn't much for fantasy, for dreams beyond what he can see and kill, but in here he doesn't have much choice, so when his hearts slow, Sax wonders.

With the Cavignum, the planet Aspicis' great power plant and the source of energy for his current prison, compromised, there's a chance that right now Bas is launching an attack on the Meridia, which Sax is trapped inside. Evva, an older, larger Oratus and the leader of the force both Sax and Bas joined, would be acting on her plan, throwing her forces into an assault that could change all of civilization.

The attack will likely get everyone killed and change nothing at all, but Sax can't take that stance. He's been bred not to fail, not to consider losing once a mission begins. He must fight to the last end, always striving for the goal. Before, the Chorus dictated that objective, and Sax, as a member of the Vincere, carried out the orders without a thought to a mission's broader purpose or its effect on the galaxy at large.

Now Sax centers himself on his pair. Factions change, worlds and space stations trade out for one another, but there is only one pair.

He has to get out of here. For Bas.

As if hearing his thoughts, there's a light clicking and a series of hisses from above as the locks sealing Sax inside decompress and the hatch, the only way out of this room, swings up and open. Sax looks, not knowing what to expect, and bright light keeps him blinded. His vents, the slits in Sax's long torso that feed his hungry muscles with air, take in the smells of life. Creatures are up there, and they don't smell of dirt, of sweat and service. Higher officials, then, coming to gawk at their prisoner.

The white glow shifts to a cerulean shade, the color of Aspicis' sky, and a low-glowing band around Sax's waist changes to match. As it does, Sax's metal plates and claws tug too, a change in his localized gravity that sends Sax floating up from the floor and towards the opening on top. Sax is an awkward monster, and he has to help the ring bring his body through the hatch, but with scrabbles and contortions, the Oratus gets himself through.

Most Meridia levels are tall, four or five meters high to allow for the variety of species, including Oratus that come marching through its halls, and this level is double that to account for the prisoners. Sax emerges from his cell into a black and red space, the latter's bright color sectioning the various cells that Sax is now hovering over. Most are dark, but a few, like his, have a white-blue halo around the top.

Sax's view of the other cells vanishes quick, however, as sealing walls rise to cut Sax off from the rest of the level. Escape prevention, private interrogations, all sorts of devious deeds would be possible without prying eyes. The walls are the same black, shiny tile used everywhere else, and Sax bets the Amigga can run current through those tiles to stun or kill anyone stupid enough to try an escape.

The first priority in a new, hostile space is target identification, followed by target elimination. Sax figures his death is imminent, and making that death expensive is the best move he's got.

The ring around his waist keeps Sax moving until he's closer to the level's ceiling, which leaves his talons a meter off of the floor. Without leverage, all Sax can do is wave his tail around, and when he sees his target, he stops. A single tail whip isn't going to do much to the mirrored Oratus waiting with a miner drawn and ready to deliver an instant execution.

"I beat you already, didn't I?" Sax hisses at the Oratus, whose scales would blend in more fully with the light, but whose recent scars leave long lines of puckered red and pink through his reflective coating.

Sax gave Kah those scars, and it's always fun to remind your enemies that you won. Sax would go even further, remind Kah about every thrashing blow delivered outside of the mag-lev train station in the vine jungles of Aspicis, but it seems like a waste of energy. Kah's not worth it.

"Is that why you're floating in our prison?" Kah hisses a reply.

"I gave myself up."

"Nobody cares," Kah says, but there's a sigh that whistles out of his vents. "But as you surrendered once, perhaps you'll consider doing it again."

A deal. This wouldn't be Kah's idea, then. No three-letter Oratus would strike a bargain with a captive. Better to eliminate the threat and move on to other things, especially when that threat is Sax, who, given any freedom, will take every possible measure of revenge.

"Speak," Sax hisses.

"I was going to," Kah replies. "You don't have any right to command me here."

"They've kept you locked up in here too long. You don't know how to threaten someone properly."

"I don't need to threaten you." Kah gestures with the miner, as if the weapon's going to do his job for him.

"If you're just going to shake that miner, then at least give me a Flaum to scratch. I've gone too long without a real meal."

Kah gives Sax a hissing laugh for his trouble. "Your pair and that mass of prey are preparing to launch an attack on the Meridia. They will lose."

The words clear up Sax's fog. He didn't know whether the attack had started yet, whether Bas and the others had made it free from the Cavignum after Sax's gambit. Kah just confirmed both. Sax hopes a razor grin he can't repress doesn't give it away.

Kah, though, isn't watching him. Instead, the Oratus is glancing further back through the level. Kah's looking through the one side of the square cell that didn't rise, and while Sax doesn't have a view to what Kah's looking for, he can guess.

Mirrored Oratus always have masters.

"If you come out against the assault, if you help us turn their forces to our side," Kah turns back to Sax, his voice a low rasp, "the Chorus is willing to guarantee your life, along with your pair's. Your crimes will be forgiven, and you will have a choice of returning to Solis or choosing a planet of your desiring on which to retire."

Retire. Few Oratus get that chance, and the ones that do only receive it because of crippling injury. Any Oratus that can fight would, will, wants to fight. That is their purpose. That is their calling. Despite his life being tied to the idea, Sax snorts at the word before he considers what Kah even said.

"Perhaps," Kah allows at Sax's sound—he would understand, too, the insult in the idea of retirement. "We could arrange for a strategic post. Someplace where you could find plenty of entertainment."

Meaning things to slaughter. This would be better, except Kah's offer comes with a deal-killer: Sax isn't going to turn against his pair, against his former commander Evva and the cause he's joined. Not to go back to the Chorus and their pack of traitorous manipulators.

"You already know my answer," Sax says.

Kah glares in response. Matches Sax's eyes for a long moment before the mirrored Oratus dips his head in a nod that, Sax thinks, carries a tiny bit of respect with it.

"There is no other offer," Kah replies, though the words come rote; a question whose answer is known, which must nonetheless be asked. "Accept, or you will never see Bas again."

Her name this time. A sweetener, and if Sax were a weaker species, he might fall into the trap of possibilities; imagined futures laid out before him with a single, simple *yes* dividing their brilliant promise from his miserable present.

"There is no other answer," Sax says. "I will not betray her."

Again the nod. This time, though, Kah's motion is joined by a whirring noise from beyond the cell. The sound of micro-jets pulsing up, sending their cargo this way. Sax has sent the signal, and now he's going to see what the Chorus cares to do in response. Maybe they slaughter him here. More likely the Chorus will use the opportunity; a staged execution for all the galaxy to see. It's how traitors ought to be dealt with.

Sax has seen plenty of them himself. And cheered along with the rest of the Vincere when those dissidents were brought to fatal justice.

Kah steps across the room, behind Sax, as a pair of Flaum guards enter through the opening Kah's been glancing toward this entire time. These aren't average Flaum, small furry creatures with a penchant for squeaky conversation. No, these are armored in Chorus blue, carrying assault miners in their hands with secondary weapons attached around their waists. They stare at Sax with fierce focus that impresses the Oratus. If the average Vincere Flaum possessed this level of grit, it's possible the Oratus wouldn't be needed at all.

"So you *are* bringing me dinner," Sax hisses anyway, because it's more fun to keep the prey unbalanced.

"Quiet," Kah says from behind Sax. "This isn't time for games."

And when what's following the Flaum, when the source of those micro-jets, slides into the room, Sax can only agree.

3 / A FAREWELL

"What was it like?" I ask Malo later, when it seems like the two of us will go uninterrupted for a brief speck of time. "With Ignos, and the Sevora?"

Malo's slow in answering that question and I understand why—back when I'd been the only one with a Sevora in my mind, even coming up with the words to describe how it feels to have something else inside you was a struggle. And that's when Ignos was trying to help me.

"At first it was like this," Malo says, and he's looking away from me, over towards the wall, but he's not really seeing the cold steel there either. "I woke up in a strange room with Flaum coming and going. I noticed their badges right away, and knew I'd been taken."

The furry Sevora captives had made sure Malo was healthy, to some degree, before doing anything else. Malo expected to be taken right away, but instead they ran him through strange machines. With miners and guards, Sevora scientists had poked and prodded Malo until, one morning, a green-shaded Whelk oozed into his room and told him it was time.

"I wanted to fight, but Kaishi, there was nothing I could do," Malo says, his fists clasping and releasing. "Every time I tried to do something they didn't order, they'd shoot me. I spent a lot of time stunned, waiting to die."

That's not what happened, though. Instead, the Sevora hustled Malo off to one of the big birthing centers, where rectangular pools full of dark ink swirled as lines of captive species waited to receive their Sevora hosts under heavy guard. The Flaum took Malo to one end, to a smaller pool with no line.

"Meant for special Sevora, or so they told me," Malo continues. "I went right up to the edge and looked over, said a prayer, and with their miners aiming at my back, stepped in."

The first touch of a Sevora on the mind is like the fading remnants of a dream—something else present in your consciousness, something that isn't quite real. Unlike the dream, though, the Sevora never go away. With me, I could feel Ignos' thoughts, its frustration as it tried and failed to crack my neural code and take complete control of my body. With Malo, the loss of himself was almost instant.

"As if I was a series of locks, and I could feel it picking me apart one by one," Malo says. "My arms, fingers, legs, then my eyes and mouth. Then I was a visitor in myself."

I want to continue, because I can tell that Malo's still broken from that experience and I want to fix him. Or at least try. When my room's door opens, though, and Viera's there, her face tells us our time is up.

"Can you walk?" Viera says to me.

"I think so?"

"Good, because Kolas says it's time to say goodbye."

Getting out of the sponge bed is my first big test. After fighting my way onto and off of the Sevora homeworld, into and then through an entire seed ship, it's disconcerting to try and stand only to fall over when my legs fail to balance. Malo catches me, holds me steady while Lan watches from the entry.

"We'll wait for you," the Oratus says. "Take the time you need."

"Suppose their sense of urgency is gone now that the Sevora are dead," Malo says.

Maybe, but I get a different feeling from the lingering stare Lan gives me before she leaves. I was the one, after all, who killed her pair. Who drove a metal shaft through the Sevora that'd taken up residence in Gar's mind. I don't feel hate from Lan, but then, I don't feel much of anything from her.

"What is an Oratus like when they lose their pair?" I ask Malo as we make our way from my room.

"I think they'd be like us," Malo says, "when we lose someone we love."

We're in a medical wing, as there are plenty of other rooms near mine whose occupants are making a variety of groaning, gasping, or chittering noises. Drones flit and wheel across the floor, trundling into and out of those same rooms, with a sharper shout or sudden, happy sigh as evidence of their work. Outside of each chamber, covering the spaces between, are large panels showing names and colored bars with values for things I don't understand.

I look at mine, and it's all blank. Only my name, in luminous green, sits at the top. All of my bars are deep black and gray. Zeros abound. According to this thing, I'm dead.

"Won't be like that for the next one," says a gravel-squeak behind me, and we turn to see an older Flaum looking around us to my screen. "We learned a lot about humans from the three of you. All about your insides, how they're juicy. Plenty of things would be happy to have you for a snack."

"Uh, thanks?" I offer as Malo recoils. "Who are you?"

"Your doctor, such as it is," the Flaum, who's wearing a soft blue mask around his fur, shrugs. "All I'm here for is to make sure the robots keep things on schedule, lend a hand if one of'em loses their minds."

"Robots can lose their minds?"

"They can rot like anything else," the Flaum says. "Throw a new situation at them, like you, and they'll have no idea what to do. So I step in, teach'em that you're a carbon-based creature and need some good old red blood to survive."

I've already thanked the Flaum, so the best I can think of to do is give the creature a nod. The Flaum, though, doesn't seem to want to stop and reaches out with his clawed hand, tracing a line across my stomach and up towards my heart until I grab the offending limb and hold it.

"Sorry," the Flaum says, looking at his trapped hand. "Just remembering where we fixed you. The new parts should be better than your old ones. You're welcome."

Before I can respond, the Flaum slips his hand free of mine, wheels to another room and stomps away, leaving Malo and I staring after him.

"Better than the old ones?" I ask Malo, hoping the Charre warrior paid attention when the Flaum was fixing me.

"Like Ferrolite said, they grew everything," Malo looks away, shakes his head. "I don't understand how, or what happened, but they said you were dead and now you're back."

I could press him for more, but there's pain in those eyes, frustration. I know it too—ignorance breeds anger, despair, and worse. So I drop it, resolve to ask Ferrolite later, or maybe T'Oli. The Ooblot seems like it would know about this.

We leave the medical wing through what appears to be a sheet of glass, one that shimmers as we approach and, when we walk through, leaves my skin, mouth, and eyes with a tingling feeling.

"You get used to it," Malo says as we continue on. "They're everywhere on the ship. T'Oli calls them purifiers, says they keep us all from infecting everyone else."

One more miracle to add to the list.

"If we can get things like this, the Chorus might not be that bad," I say. "I don't trust the Amigga, but this would save so many lives. Every summer, we lose so many to sickness."

Malo doesn't reply as we walk down the long hallway. It's wide and crowded with passing drones and myriad species. While the Sevora leaned into Flaum and Whelk, species I assume they could control, maybe even breed with little effort, the Vincere are a more diverse bunch. Groups of trunk-like Teven pass by, their carapaces ornamented with all sorts of designs, and larger, rock-like monsters roam, carrying materials or sporting large harnesses covered in what look like tools.

Noises abound too—from overhead commands issued in all manner of slang to general chatter to the hissing, whooshing of doors, machines, and generators hidden behind wall panels around us.

I'd thought Damantum, the capitol of my chosen people and home to teeming thousands with their markets, cook-fires, fights and celebrations, was noisy. Here, though, in the metal confines of Kolas' ship, the sound presses around me, close, constant, compressing.

Before long, a floating drone not much larger than my head whips out in front of us, a fire-blue light glowing on its top. It darts our way fast enough for Malo to slide himself in front of me, only for the drone to hover to a sudden stop mere centimeters away from Malo's nose.

I look at the machine over Malo's shoulder as it runs its light across our faces.

"Kaishi, Malo," the drone says our names, munching over each syllable in its monotone. "You're requested on the funeral deck."

"That's where we're going," Malo says.

"I'm here to make sure you go the right way," the drone replies. "Follow me, please."

"Apparently I'm too slow," I whisper to Malo as we pick up the pace, shuffling after the drone.

"It's my fault," Malo says. "We should have been going faster from the start. I just didn't want to rush you."

"It's not like Gar is going anywhere."

Malo gives me a look that says he's not a fan of casual conversation about the dead, but at this point, with what I've been through, politeness is not at the top of my agenda. Gar, through the Sevora taking his mind, did try to kill me, after all.

The drone doesn't take any detours or linger in front of other diversions, instead shuttling us to the rear of the ship, where a lift whose doors are coated in a mournful blue-black and speckled with stars awaits. Past the lift, our grand corridor closes in on a huge set of sealed, thick slabs plastered over with alarming signs beneath inset gold lettering claiming the engines lie beyond.

"Funeral Deck," Malo reads the control panel outside the lift. "Guess this is the place."

"Thanks, uh, robot," I say to the drone, which gives a quick beep and blasts away, no doubt motoring to some other lost souls.

The lift pushes us a short way up, and the doors open into the quietest place I've been on the ship. The Funeral Deck isn't a large space; Lan and Kolas hunch with their three-meter height, but it's wide enough to hold the members for Gar's last goodbye.

What the Funeral Deck does have, though, is a somber wonder. All of the panels—floors and walls—are painted over in deep blues, so close to black that the difference shows like a secret: subtle, slight. Whirling across these panels are faded yellow swirls, spinning collections of starbursts tracing out long patterns around us.

Viera's already here, and her eyes light up with a suppressed smile when she notices we've arrived to give her some company amid the two Oratus and a smattering of other species, all of which are decked out in uniforms and gear that make my simple hospital shift seem small. Guess being the envoy for humanity still can't get me a good outfit.

Beyond the crowd stands the real highlight; a shielded window into sparkling space itself. Along the window's bottom edge, a white-orange glow flickers, a light whose origin perplexes me until Viera whispers that it's the engines, that she'd stood staring at it, brows raised in curiosity, until Kolas told her.

"Thanks for sparing me the question," I reply.

"Everyone's here?" Kolas glances around the chamber, lingers his imposing, scarred, rust-colored visage on us for a long moment. "Then begin."

There's no hint as to who Kolas is talking to; nobody jumps to attention, there's no affirmative or beep of acknowledgment, but from the way everyone starts to move, I gather Kolas pulled some trigger.

I don't know what an Oratus funeral entails, and given the ferocity with which the creatures fight, I have to believe there's plenty of these that go on without bodies of any kind to bid farewell. On Earth, in Damantum or the jungle, we would bury or burn those who fell, depending on time and ceremony.

Without any guide, I follow what the Oratus and others do. First, we crowd up to the window, staying silent. Lan stands apart in the center, with Kolas cloaking her and using his bulk to guarantee her space. We line up on their right. Lan's not crying—if Oratus are even capable of such things—instead, she stares ahead resolute.

Outside, there's nothing to look at except the black. Then a small white-silver shape drifts into view. It doesn't take a close-up analysis to figure that it's Gar. The Oratus is tiny from this far away, but clear. Someone's coated Gar's scales in the white, and his claws have been clasped in front of his body, his talons folded up and in. His tail, though, is free and frozen in the vacuum.

Words don't come. Silence sits heavy as we all watch the figure, until some timer hits its mark and the ship's engines flare. All of a sudden the low, steady white-orange burns into a galvanized alabaster blaze that engulfs most of what we can see, Gar included.

Except, no. The Oratus is there. First as a black outline in the white nova, then as a fluorescent rainbow of color. Gar's glow hollows out its own place in the engine wash, like a star against a monotone sky.

The engines die as suddenly as they come up, and Gar's luminescence has its own stage to shine on. His body blinks between shades, crossing from deep pink to bright red to blue and back again, and as it does so, Gar's shape diffuses and spreads. A cloud that gradually grows and dims, floating away into eternity.

. . .

"For all the miracles they have," Viera says back in my room. "That was the most impressive thing I've seen yet. When I go, that's the kind of send-off I want."

"If I can make it happen, I will," I say, without adding that I'd want the same for myself.

"You think I'll go before you?" Viera's leaning against the wall near my door, as if she's wanting to ditch out at the nearest moment. Malo's back at his usual post next to the great red sponge. "Lots more people want your head than mine."

"Who wants my head? The Sevora are all dead."

"Just wait," Viera says. "Once word gets out you're the Amigga's new favorite, somebody's going to want you gone."

"Then they'll be disappointed." Malo has his steadiness back.

On the seed ship, I'd thought him broken, but it seems like he might come out of this intact.

"Malo," I interject. Then stop. Why come out against that? Why chide my friend for being protective? "Thank you."

Viera's nodding too. "I don't like conceding points to a Charre, but Malo's right. We've already taken on an entire species and won, Kaishi. Anyone that comes after us, they'll lose."

Though with the Sevora gone, I'm not sure who that's going to be.

"You didn't have a choice." Lan meets me in the ship's mess hall, a wide space where the floor is dotted with white splotches that rise up to accommodate whomever moves over them. "Gar died fighting."

It's crowded in here; everyone getting their last shot at nutrient goop and other food before Kolas' leap countdown hits zero. By my guess we have about an hour, which I hope is enough time to talk with Lan before folding the galaxy in two makes mash of my insides.

Father always made the effort to talk, to reach out to any member of our tribe that dealt with loss. He would bring gifts to their home, promise help collecting a harvest or cooking their meals if that was necessary. The acts were small, but I always caught the appreciation on those faces when they saw Father afterwards.

I also saw Father himself, how he seemed more full, more sure of his choices after making peace.

But what Lan says confuses me. Gar did die fighting, but it was me the Oratus was going after, and I don't think Lan means . . .

"The Sevora," Lan continues, maybe realizing that I'm not following. "Gar would have resisted every attempt by the Sevora to control his body. The only reason you survived was because the Sevora hadn't won. Not that early."

I'm a little offended that Lan doesn't think I could win that fight, but she's probably right, and I'm here to offer support, not talk up my own combat prowess.

"I'm still sorry, Lan. If there had been another way, I would have tried it."

Lan hisses, and I'm not sure if it's a laugh or a sigh. "Oratus are weapons. We are designed to fight until we break. It's always a matter of when, not if."

"Like all of us."

Lan nods, then cocks her head to the side, fixing me in her left eye. "Do you know how an Oratus finds their pair?" Lan says, her yellow iris sharp against her glittering emerald scales.

I shake my head and Lan launches into a story that's as much catharsis as anything. I listen, though, because it's also fascinating: there's a stretch of land on a planet, hatcheries, and only those Oratus that make it to the top of a mountain together find their way to the Vincere. Gar and Lan sliced and slashed their way through a jungle, up that mountain and through a ruined base to make it there.

"He chose my name, as I chose his," Lan says. "Everything I am, he made. Everything he was, came from me."

"What will you do now?"

"Serving the Vincere is everything I know," Lan replies. "Oratus are rarely freed from that obligation, the debt we owe the Amigga for our lives."

"So you'll stay here, with Kolas?"

"For now."

Lan shoves the rest of the nutrient goop in her mouth, rises and gives me a silent goodbye with her eyes. The countdown continues in the background, and it's getting low enough now, so I wave Malo over —I asked him to let me have this moment with Lan alone—and my friend helps me back to my room, where we set ourselves up for the leap.

Coreward. To the Chorus.

4 / THE ENEMY

It's hard to get around if you have no limbs at all. Amigga, being large sensory orbs with acidic skin, have no legs, no arms, no way to propel themselves from place to place without the assistance of some sort of device or unlucky species. Sax isn't sure if Amigga evolved or modified themselves to be like this, or if they subsisted on their own planet through their ability to grow and intertwine themselves into just about anything. Go to a space station run by an Amigga, and you'd find the creature at the center, its nerve tissue wrapped around every system keeping the station running.

Go to the center of the Chorus and you'd find the First Chair, the Amigga dictating what comes up for discussion, which species get annihilated, and what to do with traitors like Sax.

The First Chair has an exoskeleton worthy of its position: nine black-gold rings loop around its body from a few millimeters away. Those spaced rings are matched by a set pressed against the First Chair's skin, ones Sax guesses provide the magnetic latch keeping the outer rings in place. Those outer bands aren't for show either—fixed to them are a series of micro-jets keeping the creature aloft, and, if Sax is guessing right, pin-point miners. As if the First Chair is a planet orbited by tiny, deadly moons.

The living array floats into the room behind its Flaum guards, moving slow enough for Sax to analyze, dissect, and dismiss the creature. The miners seem too small to pack enough power to kill Sax, and a single tail whip would interrupt the flow of those rings and send the mighty First Chair crashing to the floor. As is often the case, an impressive presentation hides a weak core.

The First Chair heads in front of Sax, stopping before the open hatch to the cell. Its whirling parts face the Oratus and Sax wishes the Amigga would give themselves mouths already, or at least eyes. Something to clue others in on what the Amigga might be thinking.

"Traitor," the First Chair's voice comes in hard, metallic. "Why have you failed your creators?"

Ah. So it's this line of inquiry. The Amigga: always hunting for easy answers to questions that don't have them.

"Because my creators failed me," Sax hisses.

"Did we? I thought we gave you everything; life, purpose, and all you needed for support."

"You gave me *your* purpose. You never let us find our own."

Sax is hissing these replies, but the words feel strange. Ever since meeting Rav in orbit above Solis, Sax has had to use a different sort of vocabulary. Speaking in terms not solely focused on killing, on destroying the enemy. Talking about things like purpose and reason is easier now than it was, but every sentence still tastes wrong coming off of Sax's tongue.

"Your own? Is that what this fighting is about?" the First Chair says. "Your species trying to find a new reason for being? Why should a tool need a purpose greater than the one given it by its wielder?"

"Because our wielders are a collection of conceited monsters," Sax hisses.

The First Chair's bands whir faster, the little pieces zipping around the Amigga at blurring speed. "Clearly, if we allowed the Oratus to degrade this far, we *are* conceited. However, I would say it is you and your ripping claws that are the true monsters. The creatures that come in the night and tear apart families, civilizations.

That was your purpose, Oratus. To be a monster." The Amigga floats to the side, circling Sax. "Even the changes you've elected to make for yourself are in line with our designs—metal claws? Patches of steel armor in your scales?"

Sax doesn't bother answering. He's waiting, watching, hoping the First Chair gets so involved in its own speech that it floats within range of Sax's tail. One slap at the Chorus leader would be a good way to go out.

"You won't give Kah any answers about your friends, which I understand," the First Chair continues. "But perhaps you can solve a riddle for me. One that's bothered us since the very first iteration of your species, when we found it impossible to keep some small part of your Oratus blood from turning towards independence. We devised countless ways to suppress that urge, from more genetic editing to Solis itself and the way the Vincere operates, and yet here it rises again. What, this time, prompted your awakening?"

The First Chair's stopped moving, hanging behind on Sax's left. Not seeing the Amigga makes the answer easier, as if Sax is confessing to the dark.

"*Cobalt*. A space station where we found our replacements. Familiars with our likeness being made with the intent to overtake us, to eliminate us." Sax makes sure to say this loud—not that he thinks Kah or the Flaum guards might turn traitor, but he may as well give them a chance. "The Amigga there wanted us to die."

"And your response to this was to kill the creature and assume all of us were on its side?"

"Weren't you? Aren't you?"

The First Chair hesitates. Sax considers it a minor victory that the creature is thinking about what the Oratus said. Coming up with a response an Amigga doesn't anticipate is always a win.

"Look at the Flaum that work with me," the First Chair continues, its silver tone continuing to sound like a status alert from a dying ship. "Their species is inferior to yours in most respects. Yet, they still serve. Through the galaxy, species we have made or modified survive.

We do not eradicate those who we pass on the path to the perfect species, and we will not start with the Oratus."

"I'm thin on trust at the moment."

The First Chair moves again, this time coming around Sax's right side. There's a point, when the Amigga gets past Sax's right talon, when it's just close enough to . . .

There. Sax has little momentum, nothing to push off of, but he still leans, still whips with his tail and cracks it from left to right. Those gravity rings pull back, fighting to keep Sax positioned in place, but the Oratus is strong and he gets movement. His tail arcs towards the First Chair's spinning bands, and hits nothing.

The Amigga jolts itself above the strike as all of its bands pause for a hot second and its array of micro-jets shoves the Amigga up at once. Without another pause, the rings run back into their rotation, keeping the First Chair at its newer, higher level.

The Flaum guards whip their miners towards the Oratus, but at a command from the First Chair, the furry critters hold their fire.

"A program," the First Chair says. "Technology even faster than you, Oratus. We've been hesitant to go back to such methods, seeing as computers are easier to steal than the minds of loyal servants, but they are useful." The Amigga continues its orbit, stopping again in front of Sax's face. "You, Oratus, continue to be a failure. The only insight you've provided me is that, as is ever the case, your species does not survive contact with fresh ideas. You are weapons, nothing more."

"At least I'm not you," Sax rasps.

The Amigga lowers itself to the floor. "Yes. Thank goodness for that."

A snide dismissal. The First Chair still isn't that far away, so Sax tries again. Pushes against those rings and lunges with his claws, with his mouth, and this time the First Chair doesn't flinch away. Doesn't even move as Sax manages to break the ring's hold enough for a swipe.

The attack never hits. Instead, one of the miner-covered rings lets loose a precise, small stunning bolt that strikes Sax's swinging mid-claw. The shot robs Sax's arm of its strength, its energy, and allows the gravity ring binding it to pull Sax's arm back. The Oratus didn't get close to hitting his target.

"Another try?" the First Chair says.

"Persistence is a virtue," Sax manages a hiss, venting his frustration in the words.

"Stupidity, however, is not. Wasting your energy on the impossible is a poor choice."

"Then why are you trying to convince me to turn?"

The Amigga floats silent for a moment, rings twirling. "You make your first good point, Oratus. I thank you for your honesty." The First Chair rotates back towards the door. "Kah, take the traitor and perform the standard execution. It seems we must remind the galaxy, again, what happens when some choose to refuse our guidance."

Sax watches the First Chair float away, leave the room with those two Flaum guards trailing it. Then his limbs tighten, the rings pressing his body close together until Sax feels like he's going to pop. His vents barely have enough space to squeeze in air, and his arms and legs are going numb as blood fails to get through. The Oratus sinks, until Sax hovers a millimeter above his hatch.

"Guess you didn't give the First Chair the answer it was looking for," Kah hisses, and as the mirrored Oratus stalks by Sax, a brighter, red ring glows around Kah's right foreclaw. As Kah walks, Sax begins to float after him, tied to that glowing ring. "Too bad. Your record says you're good."

"I beat you." Sax's voice comes out high, almost yipping with the compression.

"But you're going to die anyway," Kah replies. "And everyone's going to see it."

5 / APPROACH

From the bridge, where Kolas has called us to watch the approach to a world he calls Aspicis, a great green ball fills in the void. It's a deeper, darker emerald than the bright leafy colors Earth shows off from space, and it's backlit by a shock-white star that, whether by Kolas' intended approach or sheer luck, hangs just behind Aspicis, haloing the planet in a holy glow.

"Beautiful," I say.

Our platform extends in a thick line over a deep-cut U shape, inside which bunches of Flaum and Teven work at terminals or circle around projections displaying what look like maps of the galaxy or sections of the ship, *Nunilite*, that we're aboard. It's a bustle of activity that gets no interruption from the approach to Aspicis.

I suppose once you've seen a thousand worlds from space, the next one isn't all that remarkable.

"It is beautiful," Ferrolite states. The Amigga is floating off to my left. Absent during Gar's funeral, I'd forgotten the Amigga existed, but now that we're arriving at its home, it makes sense Ferrolite would be here to brag. "What you're looking at is the most magnificent world in the galaxy, home to the center of progress, of civilization."

"For you, maybe," Viera cuts in.

"For your species as well," Ferrolite replies, and it's impossible to tell if it reads Viera's words as an insult. "Once you join the Chorus, everything we decide will chart your path as well as ours. The benefits we provide will be yours."

"So will the costs."

I hold myself back from intervening. Viera's being who she is, and while nobody makes a move, and the chatter from the others on the bridge continues, I think Kolas is listening to the exchange just as Malo and I are. Though if Viera oversteps her bounds, I don't think the Oratus would take her side.

"Your civilization, compared to the rest of the galaxy, is primitive," Ferrolite's monotone voice sticks to its low, mechanical pitch. "Everything your society uses, depends on, and desires will be improved by joining the Chorus. Even if we call on humanity to assist in a larger endeavor, its costs will be negligible next to the gains your people reap from our relationship."

"We keep hearing that." Viera folds her arms. She wants to lean on something, no doubt, but there's nothing that can give her that dismissive slouch on the bridge. "The Sevora said the same thing. Didn't deliver."

"Human, without us, you will fall prey to some other species. Refuse us, and the Chorus will not protect you next time."

Ferrolite floats forward after the words, ending the argument. I'm not sad about that, as Viera wasn't going to get us anything more than a bad reputation, and besides, we're drawing closer to Aspicis and I'd rather watch what's going on outside.

"She's going to get us killed," Malo whispers to me.

"If a bit of chaff gets the Amigga angry, humanity won't last long anyway." I nod forward, out beyond the massive windshield, signaling to Malo I have other things on my mind.

Like the collage of starships appearing out of the black folds of space in front of us. From the far distance, I couldn't see them at all. Great ovals and tiny slivers dancing and darting. Others look like skeletal spheres, hanging around Aspicis with wide bars connecting focal points. As we get closer, colors burst out too—these aren't the common gray-black I've seen elsewhere, but painted in reds, blues, and golds.

"The Chorus' Cradle," Kolas announces as we begin to pass by the ships. "If the Vincere is the hammer of the galaxy, then this is its shield. These ships are the outer band, and the spheres the wall to any threat. Aspicis herself lies nestled within, a reward only for loyal visitors."

"Every color shows the ship's proper placement in a fleet," Ferrolite says. "Align every one in a parade formation and you will have the Chorus colors, leading, of course, with our chosen blue."

"Who are you parading for, if the whole galaxy is yours already?" Viera asks, refusing to cut the venom out of her voice.

"Discipline is never a bad thing to encourage," Kolas answers, forestalling any comeback from the Amigga and getting another positive point from me. I'm starting to see why Kolas is running this ship, this fleet. "Reinforcing a ship's proper position, how to pilot in a formation, shows our soldiers and our commanders that we are not a wild force but a deliberate tool."

Viera, for once, holds her tongue at the massive Oratus' response, and that's without Kolas flashing a single razor tooth.

After we pass by most of the fleet, our ship slides beneath one of the spherical structures with its gold shading. I notice the large turrets dotting the ship twist and track us along our route. The Cradle isn't much for trust, apparently. When I point it out, Ferrolite tells me each of these structures scan incoming ships, looking for abnormalities. Anything suspicious, and they'll attempt to disable the ship for a closer inspection.

"Abnormalities?" I ask, thinking we, humans, might be one.

"Mass above normal," Ferrolite says, taking over guide duties as Kolas strides away from us to direct his staff from the end of the platform. "High power usage. Weapons or shields ready. More than a few have attempted to attack Aspicis, including the Sevora. We will not be surprised."

Once we're past the Cradle's outskirts, we trace an orbit around the planet, falling into a line of other ships, most smaller than ours, as we cruise above Aspicis' dark side and head towards the light. Ferrolite breaks into a long digression about the planet, explaining its long night and day transitions, and how few people are cleared to land on the planet itself.

"So why are all these ships here?" I ask. "If nobody's allowed down on the surface?"

"There are runners," Ferrolite replies. "Watch."

As we round the planet's edge, and as a filter drops over the massive viewing shield to blunt the brightness of the white star, it's easy to see the swarms of small craft shooting up and down from Aspicis' surface. The line of ships we're in comes to a congregation around what looks like a large, square stake rising from the ground all the way out into space.

The runners swarm these ships, latching onto them and breaking away minutes later. Once they've all detached, the bigger ships, their missions complete, burst their engines to life and glide away from the planet, through an open, blue-sphere-lined section of the Cradle.

"So this is all cargo?"

"Cargo, and also those people called to the Chorus or that happen to live on Aspicis," Ferrolite says. "Information and technology. All of it passes through here. As will you."

The way Ferrolite says 'you' has me stick to the word. The Amigga didn't say all of us, didn't say the three of us.

"Viera and Malo are coming with me." There's no argument on that. I'm not leaving them, and I doubt either would agree to me vanishing on an Amigga ship alone.

"You are the envoy for your species, not them," Ferrolite counters. "We cannot allow unnecessary visitors on Aspicis. Security demands it."

"My security," Viera says, "demands I stay with my Empress."

"Agreed," Malo echoes. "We will not leave her."

I stare at Ferrolite. The Amigga may not have eyes, but it's clearly seeing everything, so it ought to know I have no intention of leaving my friends.

"This will . . . require a conversation," Ferrolite replies. "We want humanity's support, of course. But we don't want to compromise the safety of our most valued members."

"You just finished telling us how primitive we are," I say. "Now you're going to claim we're a threat? Choose one, Ferrolite, but the only way you're getting us to your planet is as a group."

Ferrolite hovers. Kolas twists, his red-black eyes twinkling as he glances our way. Is that a quiet laugh I'm seeing in his ridged face? Maybe Kolas likes seeing someone stand up to the Amigga. Maybe he's not entirely under their control.

"I will see what can be done," Ferrolite states. "Regardless, we are nearing the connection point. You should go and get your things. Our ferry will be here soon."

As if I have anything to bring along. Malo and Viera match my expression with shrugs; none of us have weapons, or any other possessions beyond the clothes on our backs, and even those are tailored outfits designed for Flaum. Pearl-green vests and pants. No masks this time, and no robes either—apparently we're going in front of an audience that cares about presentation.

After Ferrolite leaves, Kolas stomps over in front of us, his heavy breathing from the vents lining his long torso drawing our attention his way.

"What happens next will be a momentous event for your species," Kolas says slow and deep, like a rumbling volcano. "But do not lose yourself in what the Chorus tells you. The Amigga drive civilization and the galaxy forward, yes, but they do so with their own plan. Their own goals. Do not lose sight of what makes your species unique."

"What do you mean?" I reply. "I thought we were joining a group?"

Kolas flicks a claw back towards the Flaum manning the various stations on the bridge. "You are. And you will get many things for doing so. When the Amigga find a place for you, however, be wary of becoming only that and nothing else."

"Like you?" Viera, again. "The Oratus? You sound like you're warning us against doing this at all."

Kolas regards Viera with a melting look. The kind that says he's so far over and above Viera that it's an honor he's even considering her words. "The Cycles are covered in dead cultures. Would those same species have died without the Chorus, destroyed themselves in pathetic wars or been drowned by the Sevora? I cannot say, but I know most did not truly survive either. Maybe humanity is different."

That seems to be the end of his warning, as Kolas turns back to his command and hisses out orders to bring the ship into a blank section of space. As the cruiser turns, grass-green lights blink up out of nowhere, forming a path through the void. At first I'm confused about what they are, but as the lights move and form up, I realize they're tiny ships, directing Kolas' pilots where to go.

"C'mon, Empress," Viera says. "Time to go meet our new overlords."

I grab one last look at Aspicis' star as we go from the bridge—it's not the same color as Ignos, but I hope the god can see his way through to us anyway.

I have a feeling we'll need all the help we can get.

The Chorus shuttle is minimal—no bridge, only a simple set of white couches that rise from the floor to meet us as we settle in. Viera, Malo, myself, T'Oli and Ferrolite, who pauses a moment when it sees the Ooblot with us as well. The blob had been spending its time scurrying around the cruiser, digging into everything it could learn after spending most of its existence trapped beneath the Sevora sewers.

"T'Oli's my assistant," I say, going with the story we agreed upon.

"None of us know how things work here, so T'Oli's going to keep us out of trouble."

"This was not approved," Ferrolite grumbles.

"Humans like to change our deals."

"I'm starting to see that."

The Amigga, though, doesn't protest any further and instead settles into its own side, still floating along in its microjet-boosted shell. I'm waiting for the airlock door to close, but it doesn't. A second later, Lan ducks through it, her large form taking up almost a third of the shuttle's space by herself.

"You're coming too?" Viera can't help but ask.

"There is something on Aspicis I need to do." Lan sits across from us, closes her eyes, and appears to fall asleep.

Once the Oratus is settled, the shuttle goes into a series of swift changes; the airlock shunts shut, the globe lights along the ceiling dim, and the hull around us fades to a near-translucent shade.

"Enjoy the descent," Ferrolite says as we disengage from the side of the *Nunilite*. "It's the most beautiful entry in the galaxy."

"I think you might be biased," Viera replies.

Ferrolite doesn't answer.

In fairness to the Amigga, Ferrolite isn't all wrong. As we drop beneath the packed lines of ships delivering and receiving cargo and passengers, the breathing room gives the giant bulk of Aspicis time to show itself off. And, set against that deep green, the tower, which Ferrolite labels the Meridia, makes an imposing entrance.

Our shuttle, unlike plenty of others rocketing towards the surface, aims for the Meridia's top. Unlike, say, the mirrored surfaces of the Sevora buildings or the stone roofs of our temples, the Amigga crown their achievement with a glittering red-orange spectacle.

Sashes of light layer, looping from one side of the Meridia's top to the other, folding between each other and dancing across the broad black space. Our shuttle coasts towards it, and as we do, the sashes change color, shifting to a green-blue shade that reminds me of seaside shallows back on Earth.

"Amigga are capable of art too," Ferrolite says. "I know you think we're a brutal species, but look at this and tell me that we can't make beautiful things."

"What does it mean?" Malo asks as the ribbons of light swoop around us.

"The changing shape of the galaxy," Ferrolite replies. "Every color, every ribbon is another part of our collective. Even as our nature changes, we stay connected to one another. A bond that cannot be broken. One you are joining."

As a spectacle, it's mesmerizing. The white light of Aspicis' star gives the sashes a shine that makes them shimmer like jewels. And yet. The familiars on *Cobalt* could be beautiful too, that didn't mean they were good.

So why am I doing this? Why did I volunteer if I don't trust the Amigga to do the right thing?

Because if I don't, they'll destroy humanity until someone does what they want.

"This is your home?" I ask Ferrolite as the shuttle heads further down the Meridia and the wonder work disappears behind us. "This planet?"

"*My* home? Yes. Our species? No." Ferrolite pauses. "Our home planet is long since destroyed. Too many accidents, too many costs extracted in pursuit of better things. Aspicis, though, is the result of those lessons. It is verdant, and every part of it produces what we need. So in that sense, Aspicis is our home. One we've built to our desires."

"You wanted a giant metal stick jutting out from its surface?" Viera asks.

"The Meridia is necessary."

Ferrolite tells us why in stages. The first comes when the shuttle lands, when we're unloaded into a tight, blue-metal docking bay with space only for one more of the craft. Unlike *Cobalt*, where a single familiar greeted our wondering selves as we left the shuttle, Ferrolite's assembled a quartet of Flaum guards to wait for us. They're all sporting crisp sea-blue uniforms, with a single lava-red circle etched on their chests. Each one carries a miner in their hands, with a smaller one on a belt. They stare at us without a shred of surprise or the skittering nervousness I'm used to with the furry creatures.

"This is some welcome you have for new friends," I say to Ferrolite as we head down the ramp.

The Amigga's taken the front position, gliding through the air on its microjets and seeming confident we'll follow. We do, and I pull myself in front of Malo when he tries to take a guardian's leading role for our little group. If this disembarking is going to be the Chorus' first true impression of humanity's envoy, it's not going to be one of me hunkering down behind Malo's back. T'Oli, though, takes its spot on my shoulders, ready to swamp down and harden into armor at the slightest threat.

I'm willing to sacrifice a little protection for ceremony, not all of it.

"I don't want you to feel unwelcome," Ferrolite replies. "It's been too long since we've inducted a new species. There should be some celebration."

"If this is their idea of a celebration, maybe they *can* learn something from us," Viera whispers.

Ferrolite has us form up between the guards, and they escort us from the quiet docking bay. We're weaponless and wearing soft-padded shoes made from flexible gel that molded to our feet back on the *Nunilite*. I still have, though, my emerald necklace. Malo has his tattoos. Viera, well, Viera has her attitude. We're about as ready as we can be when we reach the end of the docking bay and a pair of interlocking circular doors spin themselves loose from each other to let us inside the Meridia.

I'm expecting something sparse and metal. Efficient and clean like the Vincere ships. What I get, though, has me pausing in a breath-stealing gasp that Ferrolite probably expects. The first word that comes to mind is color—the space is awash with it, a glitz that, after a moment, I track to a hanging piece of colorized carapace. At least, that's what I assume the thing is—a shell larger than me that hangs on a pair of translucent bars descending from the ceiling. Each part of the shell, like a beehive's honeycomb, is filled with a different color that warps the light streaming through it from a mottled set of globes in the ceiling. The outcome is dazzling, and if that was everything, it would serve to redefine my expectations for the Chorus.

But no. What I'm looking at isn't a hallway, it's an entry into a wide circle, and beyond that hanging shell there are displays, screens and objects housed within floating prisms of glass. Wide terminals show cascading scenes of wonders—blue mountains, shifting tornadoes of yellow dust, a volcano spitting huge sheets of ice high into the sky—that I want to stare and watch forever.

Weaving their way among these displays are more Amigga, along with scattered other species all in various degrees of finery. A few throw glances our way—it's hard to tell with the Amigga, though some I see have those eye-like cameras on their floating suits—and freeze for a moment, trying to place us in their galactic lexicon.

I try to give them a smile. Try to look calm, and not as overwhelmed as I feel.

"I take it all back," Viera says. "This is amazing."

"I know." I'm struggling to fit the wondrous ensemble—even the air carries with it whiffs of tantalizing spice—into what I know about the Amigga, and failing. "I don't understand how the thing that created *Cobalt* could do this."

Ferrolite, hovering in front of us, rotates around until what I consider its front faces me with its onslaught of wrinkling, massed skin. "Surely every human isn't alike?" Ferrolite quivers for a moment. "You haven't developed a hive mind, have you?"

"I don't know what that is?"

"They haven't," T'Oli answers for me.

"Then you should understand." Ferrolite sounds a little relieved at the Ooblot's response. "Some Amigga prefer the strict simplicity of an austere station. The Chorus, though, wants to let the galaxy's unique creations display where its leaders can appreciate them."

"Like if you had a bunch of Charre tribal art hanging around the Vaos," Viera says. "Nothing like a little reminder of what you control."

But Viera's remarks can't sour what we see as we follow Ferrolite, along with our guards, around that circle. From the outside, the Meridia appeared massive, but it's only when I'm inside one of its levels that I understand just how big the structure has to be. We walk out of sight of the docking bay, following a path littered with glowing rocks, metal sculptures of creatures coated in what look like teeth, and what appears to be a huge, stuffed Fassoth set alongside a stretch of wall.

Every so often, on our left side, towards the center of the level, the circle breaks into small passages. Each one of these is marked by an overhang bearing a pair of numbers. First it's three and four, then five and six.

"Sections," Ferrolite says when I ask. "Every one of the dozen members of the Chorus has their own piece of the central chamber to call its own. If you wanted to visit with, say, Millinite, you would go along until you reached section ten."

"Which one is yours?" Malo asks.

"I'm not a part of the Chorus. At least, not yet." Ferrolite's statement drips with the same ambition I heard in Jakkan's voice, the same thing I heard when Jel spoke of our contribution to the Sevora, and what I felt from Ignos all those times it dove into its digressions about humanity's future.

"That's what you want us for, right?" Viera says. "Kaishi gives up humanity to the Chorus and Ferrolite gets its big bonus?"

One of the Flaum guards lets out a squeaking laugh at that, though the furry creature cuts it off quick when Ferrolite whirls around. "Achieving a spot on the Chorus is about more than simple accomplishment. You must also have timing. Right now, there is no vacant seat. Only when one is empty, would I even have a chance."

"Guessing that happens when you kill one of them?"

I close my eyes for a second, shake my head. Viera's going to get us kicked out before we even join.

"Death does happen, but it's rare." Ferrolite doesn't seem offended. "More often, we get bored. As would you, I imagine, if you spent cycles doing the same thing. Amigga leave to pursue their interests, and others take their place."

Ferrolite resumes the tour and I take the moment to drop back next to Viera, ask her whether she really wants to annoy everyone we meet.

"Kaishi, just think of how good you'll look next to me," Viera offers.

"She has a point," Malo says. "There's a reason everyone on Earth hated the Lunare."

"Humans are so strange," T'Oli patters from my shoulders.

It's not until we reach section nine that Ferrolite brings our expedition to a halt. Unlike the other sections, though, this one has a massive creature in front of it, one I don't clearly see until we're standing within a couple of meters. It's as though the light—here, mostly white—bends away from its bulk, rendering it a shimmering distortion in my eyes rather than a solid object.

"We've arrived," Ferrolite announces to the thing when we come up. "I have the humans with me."

"The Chorus has other business now," the creature replies in a steady stream of hisses. I recognize the speech and glance at Malo, whose own set face says he knows that sound too. An Oratus, but one that looks far different from what we're used to. "You'll need to wait."

"This is a new species! They wish to join," Ferrolite protests. "You can't delay this."

"It's not my choice to make, nor yours," the Oratus replies. "The First Chair is well aware of your arrival, and the induction will happen when the Chorus is ready for it. Take them to a waiting room."

Ferrolite sputters out a curse in a language I don't know, then turns towards us. "Come with me. We'll find a space for you somewhere. It shouldn't be long."

Yet we don't manage more than three steps away before the Oratus hisses at our backs, "Ferrolite, the Chorus will see your new species now."

Viera cracks a laugh, and I suppress my own. I'd seen my father, I'd seen the Charre Emperor make similar snubs. A bit of poking at pride to make sure a player didn't forget their place. Ferrolite realizes it too, yells at the Flaum guards to leave, then tells us to follow it inside.

As we walk by the massive Oratus, I feel the hot breath coming from its vents. It's both gross and alien, a reminder that we're in a place I don't understand, about to join with a galactic empire that views humanity as one more jewel in its collection.

6 / THE SHOW

The lift doors open to a level Sax has never visited, but has seen many times before. In front of Sax, past Kah's shoulders, a central space with a broad white circle dominates most of the level. Across from these lift doors stand a second set of the same. On either side of the central chamber are tall glass walls adorned with black-painted cameras angling towards that white space in the middle. On the glass walls themselves, which Sax sees as Kah pulls him floating into the room, a broadcast is playing.

Cavignum, the giant power plant sitting on the edge of Aspicis' long night, glows orange on the walls. Skiffs and other ships, plenty with various flashing lights, surround the structure. Apparently it's still under an emergency guard after Sax and Bas tore through it. The sight blooms a bit of warmth in Sax's ring-restricted stomach; always satisfying to see a good result.

Kah places his prisoner over the white circle in the center of the room, and orients Sax towards the glass wall with more cameras, all of which sport small red lights aiming towards his face. Sax isn't one for chills, for nervous tingles, but being here, in this room where so many traitors to the Chorus have died, nonetheless gives him an uneasy twinge. The last type of demise an Oratus wants is one of summary execution. Not much honor in that.

A shape moves behind the broadcast and one of the panels, showing Aspicis' vine-covered surface to the right of Cavignum, blinks off as the glass wall's door opens and another Amigga floats out. Unlike the First Chair, this one has little more than a simple micro-jet platform and a harness with a quartet of small, nimble-looking three-fingered hands. It orients towards Sax and stares at the Oratus without speaking for a long moment.

"It's been quite some time since we've had one of you," the Amigga says, and unlike the First Chair's metallic tone, this one bears a scratchy whine, a voice chosen to annoy, to drive away conversations so its owner could return to wanted silence. "The smaller species fit better in the frame, but we'll make do. Set him down."

Kah hisses and does what the Amigga asks. Sax sinks to the white spot, which, when his talons touch it, flows up and around his legs. Around his tail. Latching and sealing Sax. Where, with the rings, Sax could lean from one direction to the other, could swish his tail, here Sax is kept rigid. The sole advantage? With the platform wrapping him, the rings loosen up. Let Sax breathe in full.

There's a reason for this. One Sax knows because he's seen this play out before—they'll want a confession, a public acknowledgment of how right the Chorus is. Most of the prisoners refuse to give it, seeing as their death is a certainty, but the Chorus always asks. Always gives its victims one more chance to plead for their lives.

"Looks like you were part of the Vincere," the Amigga says once Sax is secure. "Not sure why I'd think anything different, except the Vincere usually does a better job of killing its own traitors. Suicide missions and the like. Still, you're here now, which means you've got a choice. The First Chair told me you have one last chance to talk. Say everything you know about the enemy and we'll leave these cameras off. Have Kah here finish things quick and private. Let nobody know your shame."

Sax glares at the Amigga. The orb does nothing in response.

"Or, if you keep quiet, as that look says you're going to, then these cameras are coming on in a few minutes. They'll tap into the Priority Beam, sitting atop this tower, which will shoot out your pathetic death to every corner of the galaxy. All of the people you served with, every planet you went to, each of the species you threatened with those shiny claws of yours will know you're getting a traitor's fate."

The Amigga's words cut deeper than anything Kah, anything the First Chair said. It's how the Amigga presents Sax's situation; as a fact. A cold, hard reckoning that Sax will be remembered as nothing other than a failure, a waste of a soldier who couldn't even serve his own creators effectively. With those words comes a certain future, where Evva's force is squashed and all of the accomplishments Sax and Bas achieved with the Vincere are erased by their reckless choice to aim for something higher than their orders.

A traitor's fate.

Is Sax ready for that?

There's a flash on the glass that catches Sax's eye, a quick spray of words as the focus shifts on Cavignum. Tilts in closer to say repair crews are on site, that engineers are working through the software and other mechanisms to make sure operations are unaffected. The words shift again to warn that brief power outages may be necessary as Cavignum resets itself to proper working order.

"What're you thinking Oratus? Don't watch that. It doesn't matter to you." After the Amigga says the words, the broadcast dies away. "Tell me what you want. It'll be your last choice in this life, so make it carefully."

Yet Sax is distracted by the now-gone image of Cavignum. Those flashing lights and the panicked broadcast a sign that his struggles haven't been an utter waste. They *have*_accomplished something, though the sum-total of the result is still being determined.

Nobaa and Engee, a pair of Teven engineers, ought to be inside Cavignum by now. Their reedy bodies would be making a beeline for the power station's command center, where they can, where they could, control access to the Meridia's outer locks. Kill the power, and

Evva's team has a chance to enter. Black out security alerts, and reinforcements will be slow in coming. A chance that's only possible because Sax gave himself up.

That's why he's here. That's why Sax can accept his fate: he's not a traitor, he's a fighter. A believer in something better than the universe he was born into.

So Sax flashes his teeth at the Amigga and gives a long, low hiss. One that says exactly what's coming to the Amigga if, when, Sax breaks free from this white mold.

"Right. That's all I can expect from your type," the Amigga says, then laughs. One of its metal hands raises up, and from behind Sax another one of the doors opens and a pair of ever-present Flaum come out. Unlike the First Chair's guards, these have no weapons, no armor; a simple green-blue vest with the Chorus patch gives away their position. "Set the frame and let's get ready to show this Oratus out of his life."

The Amigga vanishes back through its door, and the Cavignum broadcast returns, while the two Flaum burst into chittering motion. Using small, handheld terminals, the Flaum circle around Sax and align the cameras, which chirp to acknowledge the commands as they shift their shots. The action is both boring and infinite, as Sax stews in the thoughts of his own demise while publicity needs stall it further and further.

Until, at last, the two Flaum form up again to Sax's right, between the glass wall doors, and announce their work complete.

"Then get back to your stations," the Amigga announces from its hideaway behind the glass wall. "Swap the Priority Beam from Cavignum to this room and let's go."

The Flaum disappear and, seven seconds later, the image on the glass in front of Sax changes. He sees himself now. Locked into the white platform, staring at the glass projection. The screen shifts, showing Sax from a variety of angles, and Sax is so immersed in his own dirty gray scales, in the scars and the metal plates, that he doesn't realize the Amigga's talking. Going on and on about how Sax is a traitor to this and that, an enemy of the Chorus and deserving of a slow and painful death.

Sax has heard it all before and tunes it out. Instead he focuses on the image, tries to look strong. Confident. There's every chance that Bas is seeing this. Every chance that this is going to be the last time she sees her pair.

He wants her to be proud. He wants her to remember him.

So when the Amigga pauses for a long second, Sax widens into a toothy grin. Brings in a deep breath.

"Stop. Cut the feed," the Amigga snaps. "Switch to the ground channel. The Meridia. It's the new priority."

And Sax is gone from the glass, replaced by a wide view of the Meridia's front entrance. A wide stone courtyard with pools of purple nutrient goop funneling up towards a set of steps, bordered by escalating ramps to accommodate other species, leading towards a large, sectioned blue gate. A giant, pressed in C is smashed into the center of the barrier, and it's right into the middle of it that the first shot strikes. A red bolt, too small and weak to do real damage, the shot burns a black mark into the Meridia's flagship doorway.

A signal.

The attack is starting.

Sax realizes the true significance of that first shot. It's not about making a mark; it's proving the Meridia's defenses are down. An energy assault should have been blocked by the Chorus' protections, should have been swallowed up by the barriers meant to keep what's about to happen from, well, happening.

If there's one advantage to getting a broadcast execution, it's that Sax has a perfect view as the assault begins. The Meridia's cameras pan wide to show a barrage of skiffs, large and small, converging. A number of Chorus guards, two dozen or so, turn and run at the sight of the force, retreating back towards the gateway. There's no weapons down here. No exterior defenses beyond the shields.

Why would there be? With the Vincere protecting the planet from orbit and the Chorus restricting the numbers of people allowed on Aspicis, assembling any force large enough to assault the Meridia should be impossible. Yet, here it is. Dozens and dozens of Flaum, scatterings of other species, and a trio of Oratus led by Evva's black and red form come streaking into the picture.

Blue flashes lance from the buzzing skiffs down at the fleeing Chorus forces, slamming into the Flaum and stunning them, leaving bodies lying on the white stones. Even as Sax himself feels the urge to lash out, to strike down the enemies, he understands why Evva isn't shooting to kill; those who serve the Chorus today might serve its replacement tomorrow. The only true enemies here are the Amigga.

Sax feels a claw touch the back of his neck.

The Amigga and the mirrored Oratus.

"A delay," Kah hisses. "Don't get any hope from your friends. We have plenty of defenses here to deal with them, and the Vincere will scramble air support. Their end will be like yours; swift, and seen by all."

"Maybe, but you're looking like a bunch of cowards now," Sax hisses back.

Kah seems to agree with his captive, because the Oratus lifts a claw and hisses out a question to the Amigga as the Chorus defenders continue to crumble in front of the onslaught. Now the skiffs are landing, and Evva's forces are running towards that big gateway. They'll be there in a moment, and if Nobaa and Engee succeed, that's when they'll take control of Meridia's power and yank that door open.

"Switch back to the execution?" the Amigga intones from behind its glass. "You're right. This isn't doing our image any favors."

The broadcast flips again, back to Sax. Kah's in the picture now, the Oratus looming over its captive, ready to deliver the blow.

"Ready?" Kah hisses, but not to Sax.

"I've been waiting," Sax replies anyway.

"It lacks the ceremony," the Amigga calls. "But go ahead."

"Goodbye, traitor," Kah says, and Sax watches the image as Kah squats to Sax's level, the reflective scales blurring Kah's body in the light. The mirrored Oratus' jaws open, head towards Sax.

The lights don't flicker; they die. Even those pinprick points on the camera. The white mold keeping Sax in place dies too—melting to the floor in an instant as the electric current keeping its form vanishes. Sax isn't ready, but his talons are already on the ground, so they catch his fall. Instinct works next—with a snap of his jaws and a rolling, slashing move, Sax parts the loose rings from his scales before Kah manages to take control. The mirrored Oratus instead closes his teeth on air, the whoosh of the move brushing over Sax's tail.

Sax has no mask, and he can't see in the dark, so he follows the smells. The sounds of the glass doors opening and the Flaum rushing into the room. They're yelling out to catch Sax, which is about as much as they get from their mouths before the Oratus, leaping through the air like silent death, hits them and drives the furry creatures to the floor with his mid-claws. Taking a guess as to Kah's approach, Sax whips his tail as he lands and gets a satisfying *whack* out of the move. Kah takes the hit and stumbles into the glass wall, which, in a testament to the materials the Chorus used in their flagship tower, doesn't break.

In the dark, Sax grabs at the reason the Flaum came out of their room in the first place: stunning miners. There for this purpose; an execution gone bad and in need of aggressive pacification. The weapons are small for Sax's claws, but he's not shooting at range—a blast from each confirms the two Flaum, already wounded from Sax's claws, won't be moving any time soon.

Kah gives himself away with a hiss and Sax twists as, with a flash, the lights power back up and on. Both Oratus stop, because both know Sax has the position, and the weapons to make this a short fight.

"What are you waiting for?" the Amigga announces behind its glass barrier. "Kill the traitor!"

"Are you going to shoot me, Sax?" Kah asks, spreading his claws out wide. "Defenseless?"

"Yes," Sax hisses, then pulls the triggers on both miners.

Two blue bolts flash, two hit their target, and Kah crumples to the ground in frozen paralysis—even a mask won't keep you upright at this range. With a quick step, Sax closes on the fallen Oratus and bites down, severs Kah's right foreclaw. Sax takes it out, holds it and glances at the bloody appendage. Coorvin, the Flaum who'd managed to do some spying for Evva, said the Meridia operates on bio-scans, and Sax is betting Kah's claw-print is going to get him where he wants to go.

Now there's only the lifts, which Sax backs towards, eyes on those glass doors. Have to keep watch for any attempt from the Amigga, who's staying plenty quiet now that there's no one else to defend it. Part of Sax wants to go in and destroy the creature, but seeing as the broadcast is still showing the middle of the floor, once occupied by Sax in his execution chair and now by Kah's still form, the Chorus is going to know what's happening. More guards will be coming.

Sax isn't going to be here when they arrive.

7 / OATH

I walk into the center of the galaxy's ruling organization and I can't see anything.

It's black everywhere as we leave the small hallway leading in from the outer circle. Ferrolite floats in front of me until the Amigga isn't there anymore; it just fades away into darkness. I keep walking, expecting, somehow, for everything to reveal itself. All I get is a subtle shift in the air, a wider echo of my soft steps to announce that yes, we're in a larger space than before.

"I, Ferrolite, bid you to welcome the newest species to our galactic collective," Ferrolite's voice bursts out a little ahead of me, so close that I stop moving for fear of running right into the Amigga. "The humans, from the planet previously designated Ex-Two-Five-Oh, but that, as per our new species custom, shall be henceforth renamed to their preferred title: Earth."

I hear what Ferrolite's saying as the Amigga continues through a long-winded version of our discovery in the war against the Sevora. Ferrolite seems to be speaking to an audience, but as I cast my eyes around, there's nothing but darkness. Either this is a trick, or the Chorus doesn't need light to do its business.

"What's going on?" Malo whispers to me. "Can you see anything?"

I start to shake my head, then realize Malo wouldn't see that either. "No, it's all dark."

"Maybe the Amigga don't need light?" Viera offers. "They don't have eyes, right?"

Viera's comment makes me realize the Chorus could be watching us right now, laughing as we spin around and search for light that isn't there. Demonstrating the full competence of our species by twirling like idiots in front of our new leaders.

"I can see everything fine," T'Oli patters. "What are you talking about?"

I'm about to answer T'Oli when I notice Ferrolite's gone silent and the Ooblot's last words hang in the still air of the room.

"Is there a problem, Kaishi?" Ferrolite asks me.

"We can't see," I reply. "Everything's black."

There's a beat as everyone internalizes what I've just said and comes up with a solution, then a half-dozen tuned, mechanical voices blurt out various phrases like 'spectrum' and 'light waves', ending with one louder, sharper voice, like a bronzed blade cutting off everything else.

"Salcite, adjust the room light to mid-wave," the voice says. "These creatures are sensitive."

Like Ignos bringing dawn to a new day, the room arises from nothing. Shapes begin to mold out of the dark; a long interior wall surrounding the central platform where we stand, with dividing walls separating out the sections Ferrolite described in our tour. Each section is different, presumably reflecting the passions of the owning Amigga, and I see everything from glowing terminals to hanging beasts, to a swarm of gibbering Flaum surrounding an Amigga resting on a floating dais, like a Charre Emperor of old. Two of the twelve sections are populated by hazy projections, like the ghost we saw back on Earth, with teal-colored blobs floating in space.

Unlike the ring surrounding the Chorus' chamber, there's not much here outside of the sections themselves. No fancy artwork, no homages to the galaxy's planets. Only a flat, unadorned space for us and a series of set lights in the ceiling casting a deep red across the entire room, so that it seems like everyone's drenched in a bloody wash.

"You can see now, yes?" the same voice asks.

"We can," I'm about to add 'sort of', but something in that voice tells me now isn't the time to get picky. "Thank you."

"Then, if I can continue?" Ferrolite interjects. "As I was saying, we were over Vimelia, and I was helping Kolas devise the plan to use the planet's own moon to crush—"

A short blast of static cuts off the Amigga, like the blaring of a rude horn. I try to find the source, but can't locate it before the voice that had been commanding others speaks again.

"Ferrolite, your briefing and its due accolades will come later. There are other urgent issues that we must attend to. I motion to begin the Oath of Joining at this moment, so we may deal with other matters," the voice says, and while I get that it's asking the others for their input, the tone suggests there's no option except the one it wants.

"First Chair," Ferrolite starts, but its words are washed out by another burst of static.

One by one, globes as large as my head, attached to the fronts of the Amigga sections, pop into light shades of green. They blink to life until the entire circle fills in—a unanimous verdict. Ferrolite takes a slow turn at the lights, then floats back by me, towards the way we came in and hovers there on the fringes.

I'm thankful Malo and Viera are right behind me, that T'Oli still rests on my shoulders, otherwise I might get a little nervous standing in the center, the focus of all that alien attention.

"Are you ready to begin?" the voice booms.

An invisible weight lands on me as the Amigga speaks the words. The same weight I felt when I stood atop my tribe's Tier, Ignos in my head telling me what to say. The same weight I felt in the moments before we left Sax and Bas on *Cobalt* to strike out on our own; this is a step I can't take back.

Unlike those moments, here I'm in a wide room, red and dark, surrounded by creatures I don't know and don't understand. The consequences of what I'm about to do are hazy, with glittering benefits from endless miracles tainted with the fog of everything I've ever seen the Amigga do.

So I hesitate. And ask.

"I am ready, but first, I want to know," I say, each word pressing up against the last and then tumbling out together. "Ferrolite has promised humanity your help: cures for disease, technology that will make our lives less dangerous and more fulfilled, and protection from invasions like the Sevora one we just survived."

"All of that you will receive," the First Chair replies. "With plenty more still. Remember, it was under our order that the Vincere came and saved your species. It was under our order that the Sevora were destroyed."

I feel Malo step up next to me. His face is set straight, sturdy. He doesn't put a hand on my shoulder, but I feel the support all the same. "You didn't defeat the Sevora. Kaishi did. *We* did. You owe her, and the rest of humanity, the thanks you're awarding yourself."

Malo's charge sucks the air from the room. I wonder if the Chorus has ever been rebuked to its face, here in this chamber, before. They may decide to kill us here and now. Find a new, less confident ambassador from our species.

"Human," the voice booms. "I am the First Chair. Leader of the Chorus, the twelve Amigga responsible for the trillions of lives in this galaxy. Including, whether you wish it or not, your own. In this chamber, you will understand the measure of your minimal part to our massive one and speak accordingly."

A pause. I shake my head, knowing Viera's opening her mouth behind me, about to announce some retort that'll get us all killed. Somehow, it works. My hot-blooded friend stays quiet. My cold one does too—Malo manages to stew in the words, his Charre stoicism letting him store the moment for later.

"Yet," the First Chair continues. "You're correct in pointing out your own species' efforts. Your individual ones as well. The Chorus *does* recognize the help you have provided to the galaxy, human, which is why you are standing here now. Your species will receive all that we've claimed, and we will gladly give it. If that answer satisfies you, Kaishi, ambassador to the Chorus, we would hear your oath."

A glance shows Malo's not mollified by the words, but he does give me the slightest of nods. His arguments are done. A look back at Viera earns a shrug and little else—the Lunare glides through life, taking what comes her way and this is no different. T'Oli, on my shoulders, gives me a pair of taps as if to say *steady*, then hardens into a sturdy blanket. Comfort for the moment I give my species' independence away.

"I'm ready. Tell me what to say."

I'm falling. That's what it feels like. I'm leaping and now I'm off, riding out the descent in all its scary numbness until I hit the ground.

"First, your associates must back away to the edge of the room," the First Chair says. "In this oath, you are the whole of your species, both yourself and every single one of them. This includes the creature on your shoulders."

Malo provides an arm for T'Oli to clamber onto, and then the warrior wraps me in a tight hold.

"I believe in you." Malo whispers, and he's gone before I have a chance to say anything back.

And then I'm alone, standing center in that ring.

"The oath you are about to speak has been taken by dozens before you," the First Chair says, and while its voice comes through the grainy filter of a speaker rather than a mouth, the words carry a cadence that suggests the beginning of a ceremony. "It will be taken by dozens after. You will repeat the words as they are spoken, in the manner best suited to your species. Your responses will be recorded and, upon conclusion of the oath, will be sent to every corner of the galaxy, so all will know of your commitment, and all will know of your reward."

In the gaping pause I wonder if I should respond, when the red lighting in the chamber fades away except for two halos, one around me and the other around the Amigga that must be the First Chair. It's larger than Dalachite, the Amigga that ran *Cobalt*, but lacks that one's endless fronds linking Dalachite to its chosen home. The First Chair floats like Ferrolite, but instead of a transparent shell, rings encircle its body. They rotate around each other, with the Amigga at the center, the rings swirling over, under, and around. Their motion or something about them keeps the First Chair aloft, and while the Amigga has no eyes I can see, I feel its stare.

"State your name, and your species."

In the dark, the First Chair's words come from all around me, loud. As if I'm being spoken to by a god.

"My name is Kaishi, and I am a human." I pause. "From Earth."

There's nowhere to look except the First Chair and its rings, so that's where I stare.

"I, Kaishi, submit myself and my species, the humans, to the service of a better universe," the First Chair begins.

The reply comes out of my mouth, automatic. The words are numbing. Necessary. A private conversation, a dance between me and this strange creature. Even as I speak, though, I drift.

Back to the top of the Tier, with my father beside me and our tribe watching from below the Tier's rocky steps. Ignos falling away in the sky and yet speaking words in my mind, bidding me to unite my father's people to its will. Desperate and afraid, I cling to the Sevora's words as the only rope that can pull me to safety from my own mistakes, and my hands grip the black-glass knife, knowing what's expected of its glistening edge.

Every word I speak is for my species, every sentence binding us to the Chorus and its direction.

I'm back on *Cobalt*, standing on the platform while Dalachite's tests poke and prod at me, twist my eyes and toy with my senses. I am nothing more than a trial, a subject to be examined and explored even while, moments ago, others called me Empress from obedient lips. Alone, I lean on myself, fill the void between hot and cold, piercing pain and chilling metal touches with determination, the will to make it through.

The will of the Chorus is my will, its belief is my belief, and its dreams are my dreams.

In the caverns beneath Vimelia, I walk between ruined peoples, aliens I don't recognize doing what I'm doing: surviving. Next to me is an old Amigga, lamenting how its greatest loss is that it will, now, die. That dying, itself, could be a *choice* is beyond anything I have ever considered. Not a soul in my tribe, among my friends, thinks immortality is possible, but for this one, it is practical. Yet as it bemoans paying the highest price, I look at those around me and see so much life, so much spirit where there ought not to be any. Basking in the life they have, however fragile and imperfect.

Every effort we make, every action we take, will serve the Chorus' desires, and in doing so, our own.

Marilo bustles by me, both my people and not working together to repair damaged buildings, to forge new weapons or climb the ladders to the cliffs to defend our last city against an enemy we can't defeat. There are grim faces all around, and terror's icy grip ought to have hold of everyone, but I see no fear in our eyes. A call goes round for wine, another for bread, and scraps are given where they can to keep the city going. To keep our hope alive.

For with this oath, we become partners in a grand design, and forevermore pledge ourselves to progress.

Malo, Ignos stands over me in the shimmering gold light of the room in the seed ship, and the only thing holding back the Sevora's spear from a mortal strike is the last, desperate effort of my most trusted friend, who I thought I'd lost. Malo had been taken for days, torn apart and turned against his will into a tool. One used for the opposite of Malo's own purpose; his driving love of his people. Malo fought against the impossible, and in daring to try, succeeded.

"We serve the Chorus. Now, and forever, with bonds unbroken," the First Chair concludes.

I take a breath. A long one, and feel the slow slip of air into my body. This is it. With some simple words I'll fulfill a bargain that will deliver my people from their hardships, and all I'm giving up in exchange is our freedom. What a small price to pay for the Chorus' miracles.

Father, Mother, I hope you would be proud.

"Finish the oath," the First Chair prods.

I seek out the Amigga and level my eyes at the creature and its weaving metal bands. Open my mouth. As I say the first word, everything blinks white, a loud tone crashes over my speech, and before I can consider the rest of it, a half-dozen blurred, mirrored Oratus are standing in the center circle around me. They're not looking my way, though, but towards their leader.

"First Chair," the one nearest the Chorus leader hisses. "An enemy force is attempting to breach the Meridia, and we believe one or more of them is loose inside the tower."

I look back at Malo and Viera, but all I see on their faces is confusion. Nothing to do with us, then. Ferrolite hovers at the entrance, its expressionless body unreadable. T'Oli, though, makes one move, breaking free to slither to me, wrapping itself around my chest and shoulders and drawing a warning hiss from one of the Oratus in the process.

"Activate insurgency protocol," the First Chair says. "The Chorus will evacuate as a precaution." When the First Chair finishes the words, activity bursts around me. The mirrored Oratus leap into various sections where Amigga are floating around, pushing them and their Flaum and Whelk attendants out through their exits. The couple of Amigga appearing as images blink from existence without a sound. "Humans," the First Chair continues. "Unfortunately, this ceremony and its subsequent discussions must be postponed. Ferrolite will show you to a safe chamber where you can await our call to resume."

"We didn't finish?" I say more to myself than anyone else, even as Malo waves for me to join them over by Ferrolite's floating form.

"You never said the last line," T'Oli replies. "Right now, humans will still get nothing from the Chorus. Congratulations!"

"Why do you say that?"

"Most of my life, I was kept under the Sevora's rule. I wouldn't give up my freedom again for anything."

T'Oli's pattering isn't easy to make out over the clacks of Oratus talons, the buzzing of words and hisses, and my own pounding heart as it tries to calm down from the oath, but I get what the Ooblot's trying to say. Taken as a cold calculation, giving humanity to the Chorus would mean an endless bounty of benefits, but it would also mean giving ourselves the same treatment as the Flaum sent scurrying around me, as the Oratus ordered to guard this and that level, the Whelk commanded to ready shuttles for evacuation, and the Vyphen, not even present—disposed of and forgotten. Which role would we assume?

Ferrolite glides in front as mirrored Oratus usher us from the room, their blurred forms made more imposing by the hot breath from their vents and their hissing commands to move faster. The outside ring is chaos—species are running at random as sounds, lights, and signals I don't understand flag one Flaum to turn right into a side hallway, pull another Whelk back through the entry we just left, and send a squad of chattering, robed Teven sprinting by us without a glance.

"I should be leaving too," Ferrolite's saying to a mirrored Oratus that's taken up position behind us, playing bouncer to the Chorus chamber. "Find a Flaum to escort the humans."

"The First Chair gave *you* the command," the Oratus replies. "You must obey."

"Someone's not happy playing our escort anymore," Viera says to me.

"Ferrolite got its glory," I reply. "Why would an Amigga do anything that doesn't serve itself?"

Ferrolite's protests get nothing more than a hissing glare from the Oratus, and the Amigga's reddish brown bulk seems to sour as it decides it can't cast us off after all. As the bustle continues, Ferrolite whooshes its way back to us, then starts heading down the ring with nothing more than a single, harsh command, "Follow."

"Probably hopes we don't, just so it has an excuse to order us killed," Viera continues her whispers.

"Is there ever a time you're not joking?" Malo says.

"Not that I've noticed," T'Oli interjects from my shoulders. "Viera's attempts at humor take up more than ninety percent of what she speaks, by my count."

"Quiet, puddle," Viera says.

As we sweep around the ring, terminals that, on our way in, had been showing scenes from the galaxy have switched to various feeds from around the Meridia. I only know that much because, at the bottom part of every picture, the feed's location is displayed in wide, white lettering on a bright-blue background. As other species stop and stare at the screens, I realize the banners do more than just identify where—they tell everyone watching what places to avoid. What routes might still be safe.

One of the terminals, a large one blanketing the wall space between a pair of section entrances, blinks to show a massive interior courtyard and labels the scene *Meridia: Grand Entrance.* The place might have been grand once, but right now it's a burning, smoking mess. Laser fire occupies every open space, with a contingent of Chorus fighters hanging back near a vast bank of lifts. Fire pours in at the defenders from every angle as they try to huddle behind what cover they can find, and pop off shots in retaliation.

Even Ferrolite stops to watch, giving us all a chance to see the attack unfold. It's not pretty—the defenders are already desperate, and the attackers—I'm sure it's the force the mirrored Oratus mentioned to the First Chair—aren't content to settle into a firefight. A pair of small, bee-yellow balls arc into the picture, bouncing along the white stone near the doors, and when they burst, a bright flash knocks out our view for a moment. Like a parting mist on a sunny morning, our picture comes back slow and shows, among other newcomers, a rose-gold Oratus taking apart the defenders amid the lifts.

"Think I recognize that one," Viera says.

There's no doubting it's Bas, the other Oratus that took us from Earth so long ago. I last left her, and Sax, on *Cobalt*, stranded as the station broke apart. What she's doing here, fighting against the same creatures that commanded her to take us, I don't know. But I'm confident that letting on we're familiar with Oratus the Amigga want dead won't help us with the Chorus.

"You what?" Ferrolite asks.

"She's joking," I say. "Talking about that Flaum. We've seen a lot, and they start to look the same."

Ferrolite has no expressions, so I don't know if the Amigga buys my cover, but then the feed blinks away to some interior room bustling with more Chorus guards. The shift shakes us from the moment, and Ferrolite orders us on without another question.

We hit the safe room a moment later. Ferrolite floats aside and asks us to enter, and with quick, confirming looks at me, Malo and Viera, lets us head inside. The room's large, big enough for a few dozen people at least, and it has a wide window that looks into the upper-crust of Aspicis' atmosphere. We're sitting on the edge of space, and a constant blue-tinge to the view makes it apparent that the Meridia is spending plenty of energy keeping this level stable.

Alongside the usual white flooring, ready to form up to tables and chairs at our mental command, the room houses a pair of terminals on the far wall. A couple of what seem to be static images layer the other interior walls, depicting giant vines flowing beneath a blue sky.

"You'll stay here for now," Ferrolite says. "Someone will come for you when it's safe enough to leave. I suggest you touch nothing and enjoy the view."

The Amigga doesn't wait for questions, but jerks itself around and floats away. As it leaves, the two-meter wide doorway slides shut behind it. The whoosh-click quiets the alarms, the pounding steps, the constant voices coming over intercoms and leaves me with my friends, apart from everything.

I feel myself breathe. Marvel at it. Blink and sense my eyelids brush over my eyes. For the moment, there's nothing demanding me to be somewhere, to do something, to react or attack or run. Instead, I get to think.

"I almost gave up humanity," the words are out of my mouth before I can stop myself. Away from Ferrolite's pressure and the parade of promises, relief takes their place. "But I didn't, right?"

"The oath wasn't completed," T'Oli says, and the Ooblot slithers off of my shoulders to go towards the window. "By the Chorus' own definition, you've pledged nothing so far. Of course, that leaves Earth open to assault and destruction by whomever desires it, but you're still free."

Malo's walking around the white flooring, raising up various chairs, tables, versions of furniture I remember from Damantum. At the Ooblot's words, though, the warrior stops, his hand brushing the surface of a simple stone bench. He looks from the Ooblot to me.

"Are you changing your mind?"

"Didn't you see what's happening out there?" Viera says as she stands by the window. "This whole place is a mess. They've got a rebellion going on. Why would we want to join that?"

"I wasn't asking you," Malo says to her.

"I am," I speak up, partly because the last thing I want right now is for my two friends in this place to fight over a decision I've already made. "I'm not going to go through with it, Malo. When Ferrolite comes back, I'll tell him that we would love to join the Chorus as partners, but not as servants."

Malo lets the bench sink back into the white as he steps over to me. "You know as well as I do that they won't accept that."

"I know. I just can't, Malo. I can't give us up like this."

I'm expecting Malo to resist. He's always been practical, and that side of this choice lies with the Chorus and their countless benefits. Instead, though, he gives me a simple smile.

"You know I'll follow you no matter what," Malo says. "The Chorus had better think twice before they say no."

"You don't think I'll be dooming us all? They won't torch Earth just because I'm being difficult?"

"They might." Malo nods over at Viera. "But they might do that anyway, because Viera's going to say something stupid."

"I heard that," Viera calls over.

"Don't care," Malo replies.

Over Malo's shoulder, I catch sight of a shifting screen; one of the terminals, flickering between feeds of the outside. A brief view of the ongoing battle gives me a thought, and Malo sees the change in my eyes.

"If we're not going to join the Chorus," I say. "Then we might want to figure out whose fighting them, and whether we should help."

8 / HUNTER

When you're in a giant facility full of the galaxy's most advanced technology, assuming the enemy knows exactly where you are is the safest option. That assumption proves true for Sax when the lift locks after going up all of one level, its doors opening and dumping Sax out into what appears to be a support space for the level below. Several terminals glow among the well-organized shelves of audio-visual equipment.

The cameras, the Q-Net links for sending long-range messages, microphones and other black and gray devices Sax doesn't know nonetheless strike him as familiar. So many times Sax has been on a raid, cutting through a hostile town or assaulting a cruiser and there, some distance behind or floating above on a skiff, are Flaum holding gear like this. Taking and sending the images across the galaxy to build support for all of the Chorus' various assaults.

Speaking of assaults, Sax wonders how the one below is going. The terminals offer an obvious chance to check in, though at first glance these appear to be secured. Small blue patches below the screen indicate bio-markers; scanners to make sure the person attempting access belongs inside. Out of curiosity, Sax places his own midclaw in the bio-scanner. See if the Vincere removed his credentials.

The terminal's screen, a blank blue asking the prospective user to touch the bio-marker, shifts to show Sax's face, his old Vincere three-letter rank, and, following that, a large block set of words declaring Sax both a traitor and wanted. Sax hisses a laugh—he's not sure who those words are for, someone standing over Sax's shoulder? As if they're going to see what's on the screen and immediately attack him in the name of the Chorus.

What happens next does make Sax snort a surprise. The screen shifts black for a brief moment before brightening again, though this time into a gray, featureless box that fills with a pulsing leaf-green circle surrounded by a string of numbers. Sax stares at it—he knows this, has seen it before . . . somewhere. In his conflict-addled state it takes a deep memory dive to place the juddering shape into context and define the proper reaction. Something relegated to other species. To prey. Not normally worth his time.

Sax notes the number, then taps on the terminal and answers the call.

"Sax? Can you hear me?" the voice is tight, stressed and yet packed with a sense of wonder. "I think I have it right. Don't I?"

There's some mumbling elsewhere that Sax catches, though the green circle is now still, with a neon-blue outline signifying Sax's answering tap.

"Nobaa?" Sax hisses the Teven's name, one he didn't think he'd have occasion to use again. That Sax says it now is, if he's being honest, disappointing. Tevens are the most annoying things. "I can hear you."

There's no guarantee that the Teven can hear Sax, but by the series of startled exclamations, the Oratus guesses his reply came through.

"Excellent!" Nobaa says. "We've secured a room in the Cavignum. They think we're running repairs, which, we are because your method caused quite a lot of damage and without our work, this whole place—"

"Get to the point." Sax waves a claw, hoping Nobaa can see it.

"Yes. The point. We have access to the Meridia's security systems, for now. Eventually, we won't. Before then, you have to get to the top. To the Priority Beam."

That's what the Amigga below was talking about. Some sort of broadcast tool. It didn't sound like a weapon, so Sax hasn't thought about it since.

"Where I'll do what?"

"If we don't get the message out to Solis and the other Vincere sympathetic to Evva, the ones in orbit around Aspicis will crush us."

"I'm not much of a speech-maker."

"It won't take much!" Nobaa's somehow getting even more excited. "Just tell them to hold off. Give their own species a chance!"

Before Sax can reply, the signal fuzzes, the green circle goes black and the terminal's gray box shifts to red, with bold black letters stating that the terminal has been locked. Guess that's the end of the conversation. Still, Sax has his objective now. He didn't need to listen to the Teven any longer.

If, though, the Chorus are sealing his terminal, that means they know where Sax is. The sudden chiming of the lifts on the far end of the level—across from where Sax came in and separated from his position by walls of stacked equipment—reinforce the point and the Oratus jerks himself into action. The size of the lifts means a dozen Flaum, with armor and weapons, could fit inside and that's more than Sax wants to fight head on.

So as the sounds of small claws on tile floor start to patter and the first call for surrender chirps out, Sax aims one of his miners towards the lights and fires. One shot per glowing rectangle, each one melting out in a shower of sparks, and in six shots and as many seconds, most of the level is dark. The only lights left sit over the lifts behind and in front of Sax, casting enough shadows through the shelves and stacked equipment to make a world of jagged white-on-black edges.

A hunter's paradise.

Sax goes low, tapping his talons and midclaws on the ground as he slithers around the equipment, blending his own noise with the nervous approach of the Chorus guards. With one of his miners emptied of energy, Sax crouches off to the level's middle side, back against the wall. He smells, hears, *knows*_the Flaum are getting close to the center, where Sax shot out the lights. As the creatures get close, Sax cocks his foreclaw back and then launches the miner in an arcing toss over their heads.

The weapon clatters into a pile of small boxes, which do their duty and tumble, hitting each other with enough clacking to draw the eyes and aims of every Flaum in the room.

Sax can't ignore that many backs, that many targets for leaps and slashes, bites and tripping tail whips.

Two Flaum go down before any shots are fired, and those red bolts lance towards noise, towards shifting shadows as Sax knocks shelves, throws bodies, and generally turns the scene into one of constant motion. To stay still is to die, so after taking a satisfying chomp of a third Flaum, Sax burrows away beneath a falling camera stand, taking cover behind a full shelf. His vents scoop air, his two hearts race, and, with a foreclaw, Sax picks a clump of fur from his teeth and listens.

The Flaum are squeaking to each other, a high-pitched sound that bounces around the level without purpose other than to say *here I am, come eat me!* It's instinct. It's meant to tell the squad where its members are, but Sax uses the chirps to navigate, slip around behind and towards the lifts the Flaum rode as the Chorus guards congregate in the middle and form some sort of firing circle.

Numbers still aren't in Sax's favor, so he's not thrilled to see both lifts on this side glaring red and locked. Sax isn't wearing a mask, so any hit's going to give him a severe burn or worse. The locked lifts mean the Flaum in the center don't have any excuse to go hunting, either—Sax comes to them, or they wait for more reinforcements and Sax gets gunned down by a far superior force.

But if there's one thing Oratus get used to, it's being outnumbered.

Sax takes a pair of heavy steps away from the lifts, making plenty of noise. Stops just before a pair of tall shelves that look heavy, and, with a kick of his right razor talon, Sax cuts out the corner post of one of the shelves. It begins to lean, and Sax catches it, steadies it. The metal struts groan, and Sax covers the sound with a roar of his own.

"I'm over here, and I surrender!" Sax calls loud, keeping his midclaw on the precarious shelf.

Any Vincere member would know an Oratus never surrenders, but these Flaum have been in the soft comfort of the Meridia for who knows how long. They haven't been on the galaxy's front. So they form themselves up and come cautious from the center, creeping three abreast with miners raised. The second and third rows hang a bit behind the first, keeping their eyes peeled in different directions, as if Sax will appear from anywhere.

To be fair, Sax might.

The Oratus expects the Flaum to try and negotiate, but they give their intentions away by the fear and sweat streaking off their fur in pungent waves. Sax almost coughs, the stench is so strong. These aren't confident soldiers, ready to apprehend an enemy. These are scared children, who'll spray lasers everywhere before they think of another alternative. When they finish talking, if Sax so much as twitches, they'll melt him.

The moment arrives: the lead Flaum sees Sax as they head between the shelves. The miner snaps up and the Flaum starts to screech a threat.

Sax doesn't hear the words. Doesn't care.

With his right claws, Sax pulls the weakened shelf down while sidestepping in the opposite direction, using the stocked shelves as a barrier to the few panicked shots making it out as their own material buries the Chorus guards. It's a clanging, squeaking crumble that leaves half the Flaum incapacitated and the others firing madly into the shifting shadows, trying to hit an Oratus that's hunkered himself down behind a giant, dead terminal.

Sax waits out the flashes. Lets the confidence that comes when you embrace a futile situation fade away, waits for fear to creep back into his prey. The Flaum will search now, see if any of their wild shooting found a mark. The scuffing steps of light, booted feet bring truth to the idea, and confirm the Flaum's total loss of cohesion: they're splitting up. Two pairs, going to different sides of this part of the level.

The two coming near Sax's terminal manage to round the corner, realize Sax isn't dead, then they lose their miners and their consciousness as Sax slams them into each other. Killing all of them isn't the goal—no matter how fun it might be. Or tasty.

The collapsing Flaum trigger the attention of their last-remaining brethren and Sax figures to use the bodies as bait, but these Flaum are cowards. The clue comes when the lift panel beeps, with whooshing doors a moment later.

Their escape can be Sax's, too, and the Oratus leaves a set of heavy grooves in the floor as he bounds towards the open lift. One of the Flaum, stepping in after its friend, manages to whirl and get its miner up. A motion that brings the front half of its long barrel into the space the now-closing lift doors plan to occupy. Rather than shutting, those same doors freeze at the rifle's obstruction, simultaneously giving Sax the opening he needs to slip through the doors while causing the Flaum to give up its shot as its partner pulls it back into the lift.

A good description of what happens once Sax slithers his bulk through the doors would include the thwacking of the Oratus' tail, the tripping kick of his left talon and the sparking snap of Sax's jaws as they bite that fateful miner's barrel apart, rendering the weapon little more than a sputtering bit of metal.

A sufficient description would simply state that when the lift reached its destination, only the Oratus remained upright, conscious, and capable of continuing its trek towards the Priority Beam.

9 / CAPTIVES

Outside, above the blue fringe of Aspicis' atmosphere, ships are gathering. Viera's calling them out to us, one by one, as shuttles blast away from the Meridia towards the bulks of Vincere cruisers, frigates, and more. Tiny lights glowing towards massive ovals, spindly branch-like craft, and those colored rings that make up both the defense and the safe haven for Aspicis' ruling species.

"They're all cowards," Malo's saying, next to her. "They're being attacked at their very center and their response is to run?"

"Did you see them?" Viera says. "An Amigga can't exactly fight for itself. They have no hands. No legs. Nothing."

"Then how did they take over the galaxy?"

It's a good question, but answering it isn't going to help us escape so I tune them out and focus on the terminal. T'Oli's draped itself over the top of the screen, which is a meter wide, and we're watching a small fight play out on level three, close to the surface. Bas, the rose-gold Oratus that stole me from Earth, is busy leading a quartet of battered Flaum wearing ragged, varied cloth and metal armor through a floor stocked with crate after crate of what looks like nutrient goop. Chorus forces are using the crates as cover, and it's a slow-going firefight.

"Any other ideas?" I ask the Ooblot. We've been trying to get the terminal to switch off of the broadcast to something we can use, but T'Oli says I lack the security, which is why the screen's ignoring me.

"You're sure you want to leave this room? Now?" T'Oli replies.

"If we stay here, we'll either die when the tower blows up, or the Chorus will come back and force me to complete that oath. When I don't, we're dead."

"A compelling set of options."

"It's not my fault."

"Well . . . "

"T'Oli, are you going to help, or not?"

The Ooblot bends its eyestalks around the sides of the terminal, hunting for something while I watch. T'Oli used to be a creamy white, but enough miner scars and other debris from our last few encounters has given the Ooblot a series of blackened scars along its surface. I'm sorry for that, but I'm not at all sorry for bringing T'Oli with us. The Ooblot's proved its worth time and again, as the recurring nightmares I have about the Fassoth caverns beneath Earth's surface remind me every night.

"The terminal's secured," T'Oli says. "So we either find the passcode, which, as it seems to be tied to a genetic scan, isn't going to work. Or we do what the Chorus doesn't expect its guests, waiting for approval and acceptance from the First Chair, to do."

"Which is?"

"Tear the terminal apart."

The Ooblot doesn't wait for me to ask how. Instead, bits and pieces of itself flow into the tiniest of cracks around the terminal, where various pieces were meshed together. T'Oli hardens its skin, and in doing so, expands those cracks ever-so-slightly. The Ooblot repeats the process over and over again until, with a hasty patter, it tells me, "Catch!"

The screen falls forward towards my arms and I rush my hands up in time to snag the glass as it falls into my grip. It's heavy and warm, but T'Oli doesn't give me much time to do anything with it before pattering at me to set it on the ground. I do, and lean it against the silver, square post that serves as the terminal's base.

"As expected," T'Oli patters from up at the top of the post. "It's entirely wireless here. If we cut the power for a moment, the terminal will reset."

"What?" I'm still watching the fight on the screen, because at least Bas leaping into the middle of the enemy, claws whirling, makes some sense.

"The screen doesn't have a life of its own, Kaishi. It needs power, like a fire. It must be fed," T'Oli stops pattering for a moment, and the screen goes black. "In this case, that power comes from a little transmitter here in this post. One I just wrapped up in my non-conductive skin."

"I have a thousand questions."

The terminal bursts into colors so bright that I sit back, hands on the ground and feeling a lot like a little girl, surprised by the unexpected. The colors fade into a default slate blue, with several small squares dominating the screen. I recognize these from *Cobalt*. Ignos called them icons. Here, one is shaped like another terminal, black and rectangular. Another, though, I recognize; an emerald-green ring, like the Cache I still wear on my left wrist.

I've mostly forgotten about the device because, as its former owner told me, it contains a library of the Sevora's knowledge. A now-dead alien species that's never been a part of the Chorus, never been inside the Meridia, probably wouldn't have much to say about the tower we're in. Still, I remind myself to take it for a look if T'Oli's terminal hijacking doesn't work out.

"As I thought," T'Oli patters as it slurps down next to me. "They set these things to run on a slave circuit to some central station in the tower, but if you knock them off, someone has to put them back on."

"Can you stop that?"

"Explaining things?"

I close my eyes for a hot second. Think of the jungle. The breeze through the trees. T'Oli is its own creature, with its own mind, history, and way of working with its world. I can't expect it to understand me, just as I don't understand it.

"You've lived all your life in a galaxy I didn't know existed until a short time ago," I say to those creamy-gray eyestalks. "What you think is common knowledge, I don't know. I don't even understand." This is the point where, if I was talking to something with hands, or even claws, I'd reach out and take hold of one to press my point. Because T'Oli has neither, I hope the Ooblot reads the sincerity in my eyes. "I want to learn all of this someday, but now? Right now? I'm too scared, too stressed and tired to worry about anything other than survival. So tell me straight. Can we get out of this room?"

T'Oli quivers. Its eyes look back at the terminal. "I will try, Kaishi. The terminal is now unlocked. We can use it to learn about this place, and perhaps find a way to open the door."

I give the Ooblot a smile. "See? Not one thing I didn't understand."

"Don't take this as an insult, but that was harder than you know."

Malo comes over a little while later, as T'Oli and I peruse the terminal's endless secrets. The warrior crouches next to me, watches as we cascade past diagrams and pages, flashing boxes full of information, numbers and words, graphs and pictures. I'm chasing a thread, a word that appeared not long into our scouring of the Meridia's levels: *Cobalt*.

T'Oli had us looking for ways to open the door, but when that space station's label flashed up under a list of Chorus assets, flagged in bright red towards the top in its own little box titled *Potentially Lost*, I took control. The Chorus let their terminals work by touch, so when Malo gets over to us, I'm tapping and whisking away all manner of long logs and pictures that toy with nightmares just beneath my surface.

All the pieces are here, stored away in what T'Oli calls *Cobalt*'s 'file'. There's a map, like the one I saw when I was on the station. Those very same corridors are laid out, white lines on a deep blue background.

"Those were our rooms." I say as Malo sits next to me.

"This is *Cobalt*?"

"Don't you recognize it?"

"I never saw a map like this." Malo watches as I slide our view around, over towards a larger rectangle room. He puts his own hand on mine to hold the screen still for a second. "I know that place, though. Viera almost killed me there."

"Dalachite would have killed all of us if we hadn't taken care of it first." I find the chamber where the Amigga tested me, and the central core, where Dalachite's body had merged with the station itself. "It still haunts me, you know."

"We all have nightmares now." Malo's voice says he's thinking of his own demons, and I don't blame him.

I don't want to look at *Cobalt* anymore and so I swipe away the map. What comes up next is a longer document. A wall of text that would have me skipping past if not for the title. *Our Future Universe.* It's a grand statement, something I'd expect Father, or Jakkan back in Damantum to make before a litany of promises about a coming utopia. This . . . this isn't much different, except the Amigga version of paradise includes the gradual elimination of every competing species.

"Two paths," T'Oli says, its eyestalks reading alongside my own. "Your *Cobalt* was on one, exploring biological routes. The other is a turn back. I never thought the Amigga would consider it."

"A turn back?" Malo asks.

"Look at the terminal," T'Oli says. "It's small, it can do a lot, and it doesn't take any food or water. You don't have to teach it anything, and it will never ask you a question, or disobey an order."

"Right?" the warrior looks as confused as I am.

"Now imagine you add a weapon to this. A miner."

"Like the familiars," I say. "They took orders from Dalachite, and they used weapons."

"But they weren't very frightening," Malo says. "I could have beaten any of them."

T'Oli patters out some nonsense that I gather, from the way it closes and shakes its eyestalks, means we're not getting it. Viera announces another shuttle launch and T'Oli's eyes snap back open.

"That's it. Think of those ships. Like Kolas' cruiser, but smaller, and everywhere. They could fly, shoot you from space, and be coated in armor," T'Oli says.

"That would be . . . harder for me to beat," Malo replies.

"Impossible, more like," the Ooblot says. "They existed at one time, took over planets—"

"But they're not around anymore?" I ask.

The Ooblot says no and I turn back to the report. Malo's still asking questions but if these things aren't a threat right now, I don't have time for them. The report's clear, straight. Humans aren't mentioned, but it's not hard to see where they fall in with the pathways to one of the Amigga's imagined futures. We're a test, and so far as this document reads, we failed it. Other species are listed too, and all of them falter when pressed by the Chorus' standard for success: control.

"After that rogue faction, using stolen machines, took so much territory so fast," T'Oli's saying, "the Chorus forced the Vincere to strip away all AI from their ships, and most of the networking too. They destroyed so much of their power because the Chorus was so afraid someone could take it out of their control. One Amigga, one Flaum with the right codes and the Priority Beam could have forced every Vincere craft to self-destruct, or turn their cannons on each other."

"The Priority Beam?" I ask, because there's nothing about that in this report.

"The galaxy's most powerful communication device. That's all I know. Sapphrite told me all of this, but I never thought I'd get off

Vimelia. Or invade the Meridia. Otherwise I would've asked more."

"No, it's fine." I look back to the terminal. "That doesn't matter. There's enough here to prove we can't side with the Chorus, no matter what. We'll die if we do."

"We'll die if we fight them too," Malo replies. "You know that."

"Hey!" Viera calls from the window, and I'm relieved she's rescuing us from falling into the same pit of doom and gloom we've been circling since coming into this room. "I can tell by your sad face and Malo's set shoulders that you're talking about something useless again. Know what's more fun? Counting all the ships still blasting off of this place. Everyone's leaving. I think the Chorus is afraid."

"Even if they are, so what?" I reply. "You think Bas and Sax will treat us any better?"

"They are warriors," Malo says. "They might be honorable. Better than the lying Amigga."

"So if the Chorus is scared of them and if they'd be better friends to us, I say we help them," Viera agrees. "Get out of here and do what we can to make sure they win this fight."

I'm about to endorse the plan when there's a strange buzzing sound that fills the room. A pair of panels on the wall behind the terminal slide out, and with a glopping, messy noise, purple nutrient goop slimes from some hidden pipe to fill the new basin, rushing out from behind the wall to where we can grab it. Viera's the first one there, looking at the food with a shake of her head. "Even here, we still get the same garbage. You'd think they'd have something better."

"If they're feeding us, it must mean they think we'll be here for a while." I find that second wall panel that opened turns out to be a drawer full of utensils—plates, bowls, thin fabric things that I gather must be for cleaning any goop that finds its way onto us instead of into our mouths.

"Well, if we're going to join a revolution, I don't want to do it hungry," my Lunare friend says, and she takes a bowl and scoops it through the goop.

"I never like to fight on a full stomach." Malo watches Viera and then me take our portions.

"Better than an empty one," Viera says between mouthfuls. "Eat up, Charre. You're all bones now anyway."

The nutrient goop goes down easy as we watch ships continue to cluster outside. Smaller craft are joining, or launching from, their larger brethren now, with many streaking towards the atmosphere in formations. It's a fascinating display, and one that chips away at my own resolve to fight against the powers that created all of this. At least until T'Oli speaks up.

"I believe I have found your history," T'Oli announces. "It seems the beginning of your species occurred only a few levels down."

"I thought you were searching for a way to open the door?" I ask as I go over towards the Ooblot, looking at the screen.

"Oh, I don't think that's possible from here. It seems the Chorus do not trust their own guests to do what we've done, and gain control of the system."

"So we're trapped?"

"Unless you have a better idea, I think we're stuck until Ferrolite comes to let us out."

The screen shows a space some levels beneath our own, and while there's not much in the way of description—giant black boxes cover most of it, with warnings of improper security—the level's title tells enough of a story: *Alternative Species Development*. If T'Oli's right, and the story of our species begins there, then I want to know it. I want to understand why the Amigga chose to make us.

Then I want to destroy any records of it.

10 / ANCIENT ADVERSARIES

Like the others, this lift ignores Sax's input. The floor he selects isn't where it goes, but at least this time the lift heads up. Towards the Priority Beam, one level at a time. Once the doors open, though, Sax decides he'd have preferred to go down.

If he understood the other levels, this one feels like Sax has stepped out of the galaxy he knows. The reality he knows. Machines, at least those with any moving, walking, or talking capability have long since fallen out of favor. There's no reason to risk creating a death robot that could be hijacked from some remote location or by someone who happens to get inside its internals when you can create a genetically-modified super weapon like the Oratus.

Which is why Sax is surprised to find this level packed with eight-limbed robots. What's more, though Sax is too young to have seen any of the old warbots in action, these look glistening new. The sheen on the bright blue Chorus paint glimmers in the static white light from overhead stripes. No combat burns, no dirt or rust from action on hostile worlds.

Who would store these here? And why?

A step out from the lift gives Sax a good view of what he's looking at. The warbots sport a core, a ball that looks like an Amigga fashioned out of teal-shaded steel. Each one has a number of modules attached to it, most ending in either microjets, miners, or variations on multi-tools and physical weapons meant for either destruction or interrogation. All of them appear to be dormant, and their silent stares loosen the frozen knots forming in Sax's stomach.

The warbots hang from detachable clamps lowered from the ceiling, black-and-gray striped cords dangling like an industrial puppetmaster's strings.

A return to machines like this would raise terror on other worlds, would pull recruits to Evva by the thousands, and not without reason.

The first time the Amigga built a gigantic armada of computerized soldiers, they marched from world to world, building the base of what became their empire. Sax has seen the logs, read up on the history. Required, in case the Vincere should ever run up against a similar force from somewhere else.

The warbots would stream in towards the target, an endless wave of tireless, ruthless fighters. They would decimate everything with uncompromising exactitude—targeting what was necessary, not caring at all about the morality of the situation. In other words, a perfect Amigga soldier.

At least until the warbots were stolen, hacked and turned against their creators. The first time was an anomaly, then it happened again and again and again.

All it took was one enterprising Teven, and then word spread around. Rebellious worlds started turning invasions into their own armies. Before long, and facing elimination by their own creations, the Chorus scrambled to bring back cast aside species like Flaum and Vyphen. Even then, that old version of the Vincere barely held on, and with the Sevora beginning to rise, the Chorus needed a stronger, better solution.

The Oratus proved to be the answer.

Except, apparently, the Amigga are changing their minds. Going back to how it was before. Maybe these new warbots are better, more resistant to the faults that ruined prior generations. If so, then the familiars on *Cobalt* aren't the only path the Chorus is taking to its new future. One that doesn't seem to have a place for other species.

Regardless, the warbots aren't active now, and if the Chorus loses here, none of this will matter.

Sax starts looking for a way off of the level. The lift gates are showing red—locked. No chance of getting out that way, unless he wants to carve through with his claws, and there's not enough time for that. Instead, Sax wanders past the warbots searching for an opportunity and finds a terminal in the center.

Sax tries to boot it up, but the terminal rejects his own foreclaw with an angry beep. So instead Sax uses the claw he took from Kah down below, the limb now hardening into a stiff splay. It could almost be a weapon, if Sax felt like being morbid.

When Kah's claw touches the screen, it shifts and gives Sax an array of options, including the only one Sax wants to use.

Below, where the Flaum attacked, Nobaa reached him from a safe space in Cavignum. Sax retraces the call now, puts in the number and tells the terminal to send the signal. After a moment spent staring at a blinking gray screen, Nobaa answers.

The Teven's in a room bathed in Cavignum's classic orange-and-chrome decor, though it's ruined somewhat by the white and blue glows from all the terminals. Engee's hook-covered carapace hovers nearby, her tiny arms reaching out and tapping away commands while Nobaa rotates a hole and sticks a small eye out towards the screen.

"Sax, I never expected to hear from you again. Truly, we all thought you would die. You didn't! That's great news!" Nobaa pauses as Sax struggles not to snap the terminal in half. "But, where are you?"

Sax takes a deep breath through his vents, opens his mouth to speak when Nobaa starts up again.

"No, seriously. I'm tracing your call through the Meridia's map and it doesn't look like this level is supposed to be there. Wait. Are those warbots behind you?"

Of course Nobaa would know about warbots. Of course he'd recognize them immediately.

"I think so," Sax manages to say. "They're not running now."

"That's good news for you. Otherwise you'd really be dead!"

"That's not why I'm calling."

"Oh, yes. I suppose it wouldn't be. What do you need? Anything I can help with?"

"I hope so. I need a way off this level. A lift, or somewhere to go where I can catch one."

"I can't control the lifts," Nobaa says. "But I can say that it looks like there's a long lift above you. One that could take you right to the top. That's what you want, right?"

"Yes."

"Well then, you need to get one more level up. If the lifts won't work, try going through the ceiling. You've got those fancy claws, right? Use them."

"I don't need you to tell me when to use my claws," Sax hisses.

"I was only suggesting! That's all I ever do—suggest!"

Sax is about to reply with some sort of insult when there's a low beeping noise from his left. Then a rattle, followed by the soft click of a latch letting loose. With the microjets whirring up it's not all that hard to learn what's happened. A suspicion that's confirmed when the warbot floats into view, those eight arms maneuvering weapons his way.

"Nobaa, a warbot just activated," Sax says, stepping away from the terminal and turning to face the metal adversary.

"Don't fight it! Run!"

That would be a coward's move, and Sax is no coward. Instead, Sax settles on his talons and gets ready to leap as the warbot floats at him. Sax wonders why it hasn't opened fire, until realization strikes. If these warbots were ready to go, charged and set, they'd already be active. The Chorus would've sent them against Evva right away.

Since the warbots are all still here, silent and waiting, their miners might not be charged. All their programming might not be ready. Which means the fight's going to be up close and personal.

Just how Sax likes it.

The Oratus starts with a quick step around the terminal, bringing the warbot into full and centered view. With the dead 'bots on the right and left serving as an audience, Sax sizes up his closing opponent.

Sax is larger than the warbot, though the latter compensates for its size with those eight limbs. Sax counts a pair of swords in the mix, with two more bearing the apparently-dead miners. The other four hold what look like tools or docking appendages. So, two swords against Sax's four claws and a pair of sharp, deadly talons. Those are odds the Oratus will take.

Sax makes the first bet by digging his four main claws into the hanging warbot directly to his left. Whether because these warbots aren't active, or because their armor is coming later, Sax grips, poking through the robot's metal skin and, with a pivoting yank, breaks the warbot free of its chain. Thus shielded, Sax charges forward with the dead warbot covering his torso. At the last moment, as Sax sees his target pull back the swords for a swing, the Oratus throws the dead warbot into its live companion.

The warbots crash into each other, their limbs hooking, breaking, scraping. Sax doesn't let the maneuver go to waste either, following up the throw with a leap that carries him over the top of the two. Kicking his talons—his left into the top of the dead warbot, his right into the top of juddering live one—Sax crosses behind his target and drops to the floor. As he falls, Sax uses his tail to snake around one of the live warbot's top limbs, one holding a syringe-like data-port connector.

With his tail hold, Sax bites his talons into the floor when he lands and whips the warbot free of its companion and into another one, smashing its right sword arm into a hanging bot and crumpling it. Freeing his tail in the process, Sax whirls around, ready to dig his claws into the warbot's back and finish the fight.

Warbots don't have traditional bones, joints, the usual constraints of biology. So when Sax turns around, expecting a free shot at a battered, distracted enemy, what he gets is a blazing sword coming towards him. The warbot's reversed its limb, and the swing is accurate enough to shave a long, thin slice through the surface of Sax's torso. A couple of Sax's vents sting with the cut, but it's not fatal, not serious, because Sax's own instincts backed him up.

The warbot uses the space bought by the swing to juice its microjets and get itself untangled, while Sax looks for another approach.

What makes warbots so devastating is their ability to calculate, on the fly, the exact trajectory Sax might take on his attack. The warbot will be able to swing the sword to the perfect spot, right where Sax is going to be. Surprise, unpredictability—those are Sax's assets, and he has to use them. His adversary isn't going to give him the time, though. The warbot's moving forward again, keeping that buzzing sword front and center.

Sax back-pedals. He has no weapons aside from his claws, and Sax would rather not lose those to a swift swipe from that sword. The warbot's pressing him now, forcing Sax back towards those lifts, which he could try to open with Kah's claw, or . . .

Sax grabs the claw and whips the stolen hand at the warbot, who swings the blade to catch the claw and sever it. The move, though, carries the sword away from its central position, and Sax jumps quick to take advantage. The warbot's limbs are on the outside of its body, so when it tries to bring the blade back from its wide swipe, Sax catches the limb just beyond the edge with his left foreclaw. His other three claws get to work tearing off the warbot's back plate, which rips away with a second's worth of swipes. Sax's teeth attack the innards, a bite full of metal and glowing wires.

He's tasted better.

The warbot shudders, its microjets fail, and the construct collapses to the ground in a metallic screeching shamble. Sax steps over the fallen thing and heads back to the terminal, where Nobaa's still waiting on the call.

"I'm back," Sax hisses.

"Are you all right?"

"Of course," Sax says, but before the Oratus can confirm his best route to the next level is a hack-and-slash ride through the ceiling, another set of whirring jets comes to life. Followed by another, and another. "More of them are activating, Nobaa."

"How many?"

"There are dozens on this level alone." Sax puts the numbers together—even without their miners, the warbots could manage to overwhelm him, and if there's more than one level of these things, those buzzing swords could kill Evva and Bas too. "We have to stop them."

"We?"

"You're the Teven, think of something," Sax hisses, then he has to back away from the terminal as the sword from the next warbot slashes where he was.

Three warbots are coming at Sax now, gliding around the terminal and surrounding him, leaving only one option. Sax gathers his legs and jumps towards a line of still-dead warbots behind him. He lands and scrambles up one, leaving heavy grooves in the thing's body. From there it's up the latching cable, climbing with his claws until Sax makes it to the ceiling. A couple of hard strikes push the tips of his claws through the top tiles, letting Sax cling to the surface and look down as the warbots consider the best way to pursue him.

"Hold them off!" Nobaa calls, the sound tinny and small coming from the terminal. "Engee and I are thinking!"

"Think fast." Sax starts to move, because the warbots are getting the idea that their microjets can loft them high enough to take swipes towards Sax.

The Oratus isn't moving at random, though. Sax's muscles and sharp claws let him skitter across the ceiling faster than the warbots can follow, and he circles around them back towards the collapsed corpse of the first one. When he gets there, Sax lets go of the ceiling and drops, landing on top of the downed warbot. Its metal comrades are closing quick, those swords glowing red-pink with hot energy, when Sax uses his claws to shear off the swords from the dead, grounded warbot. Because the blades are made for the machines, they don't have hilts or grips like normal swords might, but Sax doesn't have the luxury to complain.

Without an internal battery, too, the swords don't burst to life. But Sax proves their worth anyway, swinging to counter the first warbot's pair of blurring strikes. The swords are made to withstand the heat and force of themselves, so Sax's makeshift defense counters the assault, clashing, sparking against the warbot's attack. The warbot's moves aren't difficult to block at first, but these things are designed to evolve, adapt. The longer the fight takes, the more the warbot's going to target Sax's vulnerabilities, make the Oratus miss, make him lose some limbs.

Which, all things considered, Sax would prefer to keep.

So he jumps back, grabs that last bit of space between the line of warbots and the lifts, and throws one of the swords. It's a straight strike, a line-pierce that, even without the energy, carries an Oratus' strength and a super-sharp blade right through the first warbot's front armor. The sword sinks in deep and prompts a telltale crunch, a high-pitched whir as components wind themselves up without restraint, followed by the warbot's plunging collapse to the ground in front of Sax.

It's a moment of triumph stolen when more warbots on Sax's right and left spark to life, detaching from their cables and making their way towards him while the other, already active ones float over their disabled friends. Sax has one sword and his back to a pair of locked lifts. Not the best situation.

When surrounded, with no other options, the best move is to limit the number you have to fight at once. Straight ahead, Sax has at least two warbots in a line. To his right and left there's one apiece. Get through one of them, and maybe Sax has a chance to get away, buy himself some time.

So Sax feints right, flips the sword to his right foreclaw and leans that way, drawing the warbots in that direction and forcing the right warbot to raise its sword in a straight defense designed to block a throw like the one Sax just made at its companion. Already learning. Shifting his weight, throwing his tail to the right to help swivel him around, Sax pivots and launches to the left, over the stabbing charge of a warbot who thought it had an open shot at the Oratus' back. Sax's leap carries him over the warbot's blades, with Sax bringing his talons up into a tuck to avoid the scorching slices.

As Sax crashes into the advancing warbot, he uses his midclaws to clamber over the machine. With his right foreclaw, Sax jams his other blade through the top of the orb, stuttering the warbot into collapse. Sax rides the machine to the ground, then yanks the blade out with his right midclaw and breaks into a run, ducking and weaving through the crowd of hanging warbots, more and more of whom are starting up to life. Sax can move for the moment, but he's going to be overwhelmed in the next.

"We've found an opportunity!" Nobaa's screaming through the terminal rises above the medley of mechanical whines. "These warbots are still running old software! That's why they're not active—the Chorus must have known they'd be vulnerable!"

Sax, who's cutting wildly with the sword as he runs around the level, doesn't get what the Teven's saying. So what if the warbots haven't had their internal programming changed—it's not like Sax can adjust it now. The Oratus barely has time to duck and dodge sword strikes. More and more warbots are activating and the level's filling with the whir of microjets and the whine from the swords.

One of those blades will land a cut sooner or later, and Sax won't survive what follows.

11 / TRESPASSERS

Learn why we were made, and then destroy our makers. Seems simple enough, but doing either requires getting out of this safe room. The terminal's been no help, so the four of us are standing in front of the door, willing it to open.

"What if I scream for help? Think anyone will answer?" Viera asks.

"Try it." I don't think anyone will, but it's worth a shot.

Malo and I, with T'Oli coating me in its own body armor, take up positions on either side of the door, and at my nod, Viera commences with a series of truly terrifying shrieks. She howls that the window's cracking, that we're about to get sucked into space, and that I'm suffering from some sort of critical illness. It's inventive, it's scary, and I'd come running if I heard it.

Or maybe I'd head the other way.

The door, though, stays shut. Resolute.

"Guess they don't care if we die in here." Viera sounds offended.

"More likely they can see what we're doing and know there's no real threat," T'Oli patters. "I would bet someone from the Chorus is watching every move we make."

"You could have suggested that earlier," I say. "Saved us the trouble of listening to Viera."

"I believe letting loose can be healthy."

"It did feel good to scream," Viera agrees. "You should try it, Empress. You've got to be frustrated."

I am, but it's not the kind of frustration that's helped by screaming and shouting. I look at the door again, "T'Oli, you think they're watching us?"

"I doubt there's anything in the Meridia that isn't watched, Kaishi."

"Then why don't we give them a show?"

T'Oli tilts its eyestalks, which, seeing as those stalks are resting on my shoulders, makes it look like I have a pair of gray growths spiking out of me.

"Make your sword," I suggest. "Let's try and hack our way out of here."

"I don't think the door is thin enough?"

"Guess we'll find out," I reply to the Ooblot as it forms up along my hand, its skin hardening into a razor edge. "You ready?"

"For you to hit me against a door? Technically, I am as sharp and as durable as I can be, so yes. Hit away."

"Sorry," I say as I take the first swing with my right arm.

It's an overhead chop, meant to slice the door vertically down the middle. Instead, T'Oli's edge strikes the metal and bounces off, though the Ooblot does manage to leave a small groove where I hit.

"That's going to take a long time," Malo says from his corner, watching.

"If you have any other ideas, I'm listening." I try to keep frustration from nipping at the edges of my words, but it's hard. Chipping through this door with T'Oli is going to take more time and strength than I have, and that's not counting whether the Ooblot's going to put up with the abuse.

I give Malo a few seconds, but no inspiration flies from his lips, so I lift T'Oli up for a second strike. Both of its eyes wince, and mine do too. And I swing. There's a clank, a screech of metal and another piece, a little larger, falls out to the ground. I sweep the chunk away with my foot—it's barely bigger than my fingertip—and get set for round three.

When the door opens.

There's no warning. No gradual twisting of locks or command from Ferrolite that we're about to get introduced to some new guards. Instead, from one moment to the next I'm looking at a gray metal barrier and then a pair of annoyed, black-furred, blue-uniformed Flaum. Their miners are holstered, their claws are at their sides, and their beady eyes go right to the Ooblot I'm wearing on my arm. Behind them, the once-crowded halls of the Chorus ring look very, very empty.

"Hi," is all I can think of to say.

Malo works faster, flying out from the side to tackle the left Flaum and drive the furry creature into the ground. That draws the eyes of its companion, which opens it up to a swing once my instincts kick back in. These Flaum are meant to keep us here, not help us. Yet when my right hand, with T'Oli on it, lands, I don't feel the smooth stabbing of a sharp knife but the jolt up my arm of a hammer blow. My target stumbles backward, to the other side of the doorway, and its hands go towards the matted fur spot where I've apparently punched it.

"What are you doing?" I shout at the Ooblot even as I step into another swing, this one aiming higher.

The Flaum, though, ducks the move and dives at me. Gets beneath my swipe and hits my waist. Knocks us both to the ground. T'Oli thinks fast and slimes from my hand up and around the Flaum's left claw, then drips to the floor before the Flaum can shake the Ooblot off. T'Oli hardens as I squeeze out from under the creature, sealing the Flaum to the ground.

"Stop." Viera's voice hits loud and hard. "I hate the smell, but move and I'm torching your fur."

The Lunare stands next to us, a miner in her hand and pointing at my Flaum. The one tussling with Malo stops too, with Malo gripping both its forearms in what looks like a stalemate. That one still has its miner holstered, but mine is missing its weapon.

Viera's threat gives me the time I need to walk over to Malo's Flaum and yank its miner away. From there it's a threaten-and-move situation to get the pair of Flaum guards to walk back into our former prison. We head outside, T'Oli back on my shoulders, and Malo taps the panel to slide the door shut.

"Is it cruel to leave them in there?" Viera asks.

"They did it to us," I reply. "Fair trade."

The Chorus ring is deserted. The alarms have, thankfully, gone quiet. All the terminals now have a blaze red EVACUATION banner glowing across the bottom, followed by a strict sentence declaring said evacuation is only for Amigga and their guards. All other Chorus personnel, apparently, must fight for their fleeing masters.

"What would Damantum have done if the Emperor had fled the city and left the rest to die?" I ask Malo as we walk by the screens.

"They would have obeyed," Malo replies. "The Emperor had divine right. Some may have fled eventually, when the end was clear. But most? They would have stayed."

I take his words to mean we'll still find plenty of resistance here. The terminals showing the fighting taking place in the Meridia sport level numbers in the corners, and while there aren't signs saying what level we're on, I'm willing to bet it's a lot higher than the thirty-second floor I'm seeing on the terminals showing the constant battle.

Any Amigga, Flaum, or other Chorus troops that haven't made the long descent will still be here. Whether they'll take our escape as an assault or ignore us, I'm not sure.

"So do we descend?" T'Oli asks. "Try to meet up with the fighters?"

I want the Chorus to fall, I want to help Bas, but at the same time, Malo, Viera and I have two small miners to our names. We're far from some rescuing force blitzing to the rescue, and I'd rather not get caught in a firefight when neither force knows whose side we're on.

"No," I say as we continue along the ring. "We're not going all the way down yet. First, I want to learn about us."

"Us?" T'Oli asks.

"She means humans," Viera says. "I'm interested in weapons, if that counts. We find any, I get first choice."

"All yours," I say. "T'Oli, you said you think you know where the Chorus is keeping our history?"

T'Oli affirms it found a strange level not far below this one: a space with a spotty description that hinted at secrets I'd dearly love to know.

Back on Earth, I'd learned a little about the Amigga that designed us. It failed many times, and left its failures for us to find beneath the ash and wreck of an attempted Vincere extermination. But it was also clear that Amigga, that Ignos saved us. Took a shuttle and flew us away to the other side of the planet and let us thrive. What I want to find out is *why*? Why us? Why make humans when the Amigga have Oratus, when they have hordes of Flaum waiting to obey their every order?

"Something's coming," Malo, whose a half-step ahead of me, snaps. "Fight or run?"

From the growing clatter of boots on the ground, a fight is going to end with all of us dead or imprisoned. So I make the call and we cast around for a place to run to. Going back around the ring seems doable, but they might keep on going after us. If there's one place I *don't* want to fight someone, it's outside our old safe room, where a couple of angry Flaum reinforcements are a door panel away.

There's a dark entrance to the Chorus chamber to my left, but if there's any part of the Meridia under constant watch, I'm guessing it's there. So when Viera breaks for a small door slotted opposite the section entrance, I go with her.

Unlike our safe room, this door opens at our approach. No panel required. It's easy to see why—a store room. We rush in, crowd among the boxes and metal shelves holding all manner of supplies. No weapons that I can see. Only tools, slice of life stuff like solutions labeled for cleaning, repairs, or more. Powered-down robots linger in the corners and hang from hooks in the rafters.

As we pile in, the door closes behind us, leaving only a greenish glow from lights ringing the crease around the sides of the ceiling. It's enough to see, enough to make out that there's something else in the back of this large storeroom. The bright white-blue light of a terminal screen halos its circular silhouette. Malo holds up a hand to us in the universal signal for quiet and advances. As he goes, Malo's left hand slips onto a shelf and slides off what looks like a thick metal bar with a curved end. The motion doesn't make any noise, and Malo slips the weapon into a two-handed grip as he gets closer. Viera and I watch, miners raised, and T'Oli forms its customary armor over my chest.

"If you're looking for the intruders, they aren't here," a gruff, robotic voice sounds. "You should know better than to think they'd make it this far."

Malo pauses, throws a glance back my way.

"You're not a bunch of mutes, are you?" the voice continues. "I thought that gene line died out some time ago. Turns out you Flaum go insane if you can't talk to each other."

Flaum? I'm almost insulted. Malo's confused now, and Viera's looking at me with a narrow-eyed, tight-lipped stare that's begging permission to roast this thing, but I'm a curious person, and I can't help but ask.

"You think we're Flaum?" I say, gesturing for Malo to move to the side and give Viera a clear shot.

The creature shudders for a second, and then there's a whir of a machine spooling up. With a grind of creaky metal, the Amigga turns around to face us. It's not too distinct with the terminal's light washing out its skin, but it's easy to pick out the thick, rudimentary metal legs and bars forming a cradle for the creature. Compared to what I've seen with Ferrolite, much less the First Chair, this Amigga's equipment is so basic that I have to repress a laugh.

"Humans?" the Amigga sounds surprised. "You're not supposed to exist."

"Yeah, we know," Viera says. "You and the Sevora both tried to make sure of that. And both of you failed."

"No, no," the Amigga replies. "Not like that. There was always something wrong with your make-up. Your species could never live long enough to be viable. That's why the experiment was scrapped. Such a shame we had to waste a great planet on you."

"You didn't waste it," I say. "It's our home."

"Is it?" the Amigga laughs. "Of course Ignos would pull a move like that. It always was bullheaded. Never wanted to give up even when its projects failed."

Part of me wants to hear what the Amigga knows, another part of me is getting annoyed at the Amigga's constant barrage of insults.

"Why do—" I start to say.

"Be good little failures," the Amigga interrupts, "and leave me now. The First Chair calls for an evacuation and I finally have a moment of peace to myself. Can't have mistakes like you ruining it."

"Call me a mistake one more time," Viera says.

"Are you upset by the truth, failure?"

Before another word leaves its speakers, there's a series of bright red flashes tracing from Viera's miner to the Amigga. Each hit sparks a tiny flame, and at the third, a garbled groan comes from the creature. Then Malo's filling the space, striking hard and fast with his stolen tool. He breaks anything he can find on the Amigga's machine, then cracks apart the terminal's screen too.

"I don't know what's going to shoot us in here," Malo says to my raised eyebrow when the warrior's done flailing around.

"Agreed," Viera says.

"It could have told us something," I say, going up closer and looking at the Amigga. "It knew about us."

"What it knew," Malo says, "isn't us. We're not some failed experiment, Kaishi. We're the only ones who get to decide what we are."

The Amigga's body is burned and crumpled. Whatever secrets it held, I'm not going to hear them now. So I stand, turn around to my fellow failures, and nod towards the door.

"Malo, you're starting to think like me," Viera says. "I don't like it."

"Me neither."

12 / WORTHLESS

Unfortunately, the opposite side of the level isn't any better than where Sax came in from. Just a pair of lifts, both locked down with a glowing red panel, and without Kah's now-severed hand, Sax isn't getting out that way either. Instead, he has to jump and gouge off of the wall to dodge a series of strikes from the pursuing warbots. More than a dozen, now, rotate to watch Sax leap from the wall into another batch of still-dead warbots, using their cables to keep himself moving above the ground.

Running around in pointless circles isn't going to keep him alive for long.

"We've found an exploit!" Nobaa's yelling from the center terminal, the one voice that, as much as it bugs him, gives Sax a bit of hope. "Engee's in the Meridia's network, and all these warbots are hooked into—"

Sax misses the last part of that as the warbot he's standing on activates and pops loose from its cable. His talons keep Sax gripped on top, and give the Oratus a chance to leap before the new warbot swings its sword through where Sax was standing. With his own powerless blade, Sax blocks the warbot's second sword as the Oratus lands on the next warbot in line. He'd like to turn back and take the fight to one of these things, but several more are already swarming the position, their microjets floating them over deactivated machines and towards Sax. A sightless, implacable line of glowing swords and blue-metal orbs.

Back to the original lifts. Buying time. Buying space. But when Sax gets to those same doors, that same red panel, he stops. His vents push out air, and he hisses one long, low sound. Running isn't what he's meant for, isn't what he does. If Sax is going to die, it won't be with a sword to the back. It'll be fighting and trying, however impossible it might be, to live.

Wheeling around, Sax expects to find the warbots coming towards him, ready to slice him into Oratus chunks. What he sees instead forces a blink, then another. A sorting of the sounds, the clashing and clanging that Sax thought was the warbots forcing their way through to him but is, instead, the battering cacophony of metal smashing metal. More warbots are activating, disengaging from the thick black-white cables holding them to the ceiling and settling into a fight with . . . each other. Swords swing, buzzing with energy, and empty miners bash against each other as metal limbs fly and sparks set fires to cables and wires scattered around the room as the machines destroy themselves.

Sax watches. Spends a thought thanking Nobaa, Engee. The terminal's in the middle of that fiery robot struggle, and Sax figures it's not going to survive. The two Teven must have found a way to do exactly what had been done to warbots countless times throughout their existence—turn them against their creators.

It's good to have the reason for his existence confirmed.

Now Sax suppresses his own instincts. He wants to jump into the fight, to tear and bite and destroy along with the mechanical things, but Sax holds himself back. Focuses his swift-beating hearts and his twitchy eyes away from non-imminent death and towards the ceiling. Nobaa said his escape was up there, through the ceiling to another lift. One that could go higher, maybe all the way to the Priority Beam.

Sax takes another jump, scales the wall to the ceiling and digs in with his talons and foreclaws while his midclaws get to work tearing and shredding aside the tiles. Digging their way through the Meridia's guts to carve a path upwards. There's pipes and wires, unknown cabling and things that make noises as Sax tries to weave his way through them. An Oratus isn't small, so while Sax tries to shove aside what he can, he leaves more than a few snapped and shattered things left in the annals between the two levels.

Sometimes those things shower Sax's scales in sparks, sometimes in gasses or in disgusting fluids, but Sax doesn't think about it. Forces himself past the moment and into the future, to where all of this pays off. To where there is no more Chorus and the only choice he'll have to make is where, with Bas, they want to go. What things they want to hunt. The hope sticks with Sax and helps him grind his way through until he gets to the thicker flooring before the next level.

Scrunched between a thick black pipe that suggests terrible things if it's broken and a knotted assemblage of cords, only some of which bear Sax's slashing marks, the Oratus squishes up against the heavy tile. It's cool, and red. Thick and smooth, even on the underside. What light Sax has filters up from the level below, where, going by the noise, the warbot brawl continues on. He can see, he can brace, and he can push, and when Sax does, the tile buckles and breaks free of its setting, sliding up and over its neighbors.

There's one problem: the tile is small, and Sax is huge. He has to shift more, and do it before anything on this level decides to blast him to pieces. Sax works fast, kicking and pushing other tiles aside, expecting a blast to come through at any moment, but none does, and Sax gets himself out and standing without a single attack rendering him useless.

"Fascinating. I never expected to see myself here," the words are soft, slow and methodical, as if each one comes as the result of deliberate effort.

The level is lit in dim crimson from a series of lamps over the lift doors on either side of the level. The first thing Sax notices, after tracking to the light, is that both banks have red-glowing panels in front of them. Locked beyond Sax's ability to open them.

"You don't need to worry," the voice continues. "They drop the food down every now and then. Enough to keep you from starving."

Sax looks back to the sound, the weakness of which led the Oratus to discount the noise until any possible escapes could be identified. Seeing as there are none of those, Sax affords the speaker his full, clawed attention. And recoils. Almost falls back through the hole he's just made.

The voice comes from an Oratus, but it's the oldest Oratus Sax has ever seen. Scales once a metallic green are chipped and fading, curling at the edges like a flower in the cold. Dark holes sit where his eyes should be, and of his claws, only the right foreclaw remains. All others have been grafted together, their ends pulled into harmless clubs. Teeth too, are gone, and the talons shriveled, translucent splinters.

"Age is a terrible thing," the Oratus continues. "We're not meant to grow old, you and I. Not made for it."

"Who are you?"

"Me? I was someone once, a very long time ago, but now I am only a test. An experiment for the Chorus." The Oratus glances upward with its eyeless face. "They watch me all the time. Looking for something, anything. They keep me alive, use me for what they need, and leave me here when they are done, to wait."

Sax follows the look. Across the ceiling, shrouded in shadows due to the angle of those red-eyed lamps, camera nubs sprinkle across the tiles. So many of them for one subject, for one small area.

"But what are you, visitor?" the Oratus asks. "A new subject? Have the rules of the game changed?"

"The game is ending," Sax hisses. He doesn't have time for this, no matter how curious this Oratus and his story might be. "Do you know a way to call the lifts?"

The Oratus laughs, or wheezes, Sax can't really tell what the old creature's vents are doing. "You don't call them. They do." The one claw points up. "Everything here belongs to them, including you and I."

Sax is about to go take a closer look at one of the lift banks, but the Oratus' words deliver an angry cut. This creature is wrong, broken. An Oratus should never give up. Should fight to the last, and embrace a well-earned death. This one is everything that an Oratus should never be.

"Nothing owns me," Sax replies, and instead of going to the lifts, he stomps towards the old Oratus, who is lying on the empty floor near a waste-water recycler. "The Chorus may have made me, but I am not their tool."

On the battlefield, Sax would help a downed fighter. He would bring them to their feet, administer what aid he could and call for help so that he could resume his real mission. This isn't a battlefield, and the old Oratus, aside from its age, appears unharmed. Maybe that's why Sax is so compelled to force the Oratus to his talons, to get the creature standing. The old Oratus hisses in surprise when Sax suddenly grips its arms and lifts the creature up.

"Your name?"

"Subject," the Oratus hisses weakly, leaning on Sax. "That is what they call me."

"I don't care what they call you. What is your name?"

The Oratus lifts his head, a slow, creaking motion that has Sax wincing. It is wrong for an Oratus to be this weak.

"Rovel," the Oratus finally says, the letters marching out one after another like an opening box.

Five letters, and not a combination Sax has heard before. Not a name for an Oratus bent to war, nor one for command. Rovel. The name's surprising enough that Sax steps back—careful to keep his claws in position to catch Rovel should he topple forward—and considers the old Oratus again. The wounds, the deformations, but he can see a different frame on Rovel now. Standing, Rovel doesn't assume a combat stance. He's straight, his claws, aside from the midclaw bracing himself against the watering station, hang limp by his sides and Rovel's eyes track towards the ground.

Demure, servile.

"They've broken you?" Sax ventures to ask. There has to be some explanation for this, for why an Oratus would be so placid.

"Broken?" Rovel says, then pauses, as if considering whether he might be. "No. No. Not broken. Defeated, maybe, but I was made this way."

Another strange word to use, and Sax ignores the pressure to get moving, to find an exit, to follow intuition down its dark path. "You're the first one."

Now Rovel looks up. Now Rovel meets Sax square. "The first one that survived."

"They've kept you alive all this time?"

"Too valuable to die."

Sax doubts that, looking at Rovel. The Chorus could have captured any number of Oratus, taken them from the Vincere and secreted them here. There must be some other reason, maybe one that could help.

"Tell me how to get off the level," Sax hisses sharp. "Now."

"I already—"

"You lied."

Rovel tilts his head. Says nothing.

"The Amigga are ruthless. They would replace something as worthless as you seem to be. Call the lifts."

Rovel gives Sax a level stare and, for the first time, bares his teeth. "I am the first, but I am also the last, Oratus. They gave me a mind to match this body, and when it proved too strong, I helped them reduce your kind to instinctual monsters. To flashes of anger coupled with just enough comprehension to make military strategy." Rovel settles as he rasps the words, shedding off the weaker stance, standing firm and glaring bright. "You are a product, and we are your maker."

"I don't care," Sax says, and it's true. He is who, what he is.

Nothing this pathetic excuse for an Oratus might say can change that. "Call the lifts."

"Do you know why I'm here?" Rovel hisses again, apparently not hearing Sax. "Because you all failed. I used to be at the top of this tower, used to stand near the First Chair. But now the Oratus will go extinct, replaced by those machines. All because of your resistance. Because you will not obey your creators."

"One more time. The lifts."

When Rovel takes a deep breath, starts in on another rant, Sax whips his tail and cracks the elder Oratus in the face, sending Rovel reeling into the wall next to the water station. It's a move that tells Sax all he needs to know—his tail came in a long arc, with plenty of time for Rovel to intercept, dodge, or even attack Sax before the strike arrived.

Oratus should be weapons, and even an old weapon ought to know how to fight.

"Pathetic," Sax hisses, then turns towards the left lift bank.

Nobaa said there was a lift here capable of taking Sax all the way up to the top. There are four on this level, and one of them is what he's looking for. Five long strides brings Sax to the lift doors and their red panel, with no way to unlock it.

Unless . . .

"Rovel," Sax looks back at the old Oratus, picking himself up slow from the ground. "You might have a way to serve your species yet."

13 / CREATION

On the far end of the level, opposite the docking bay where we arrived, sits a bank of four smooth metal doors. Each one is shaded a different color, and as we approach a raised panel standing front of them, the screen divides to show ranges of numbers next to small, colored squares showing those same colors.

"This makes it easy," I say as we walk up to them. Around us, the usual collection of terminals occupy the otherwise empty ring. After leaving the Amigga's corpse back in the storeroom, we've moved slow to get here, but we haven't heard another set of steps coming our way. "Where did you say the level was?"

"Only three beneath ours," T'Oli replies. "So, the green one."

Each of the doors has a single-screen panel that sits dark until I press my palm against its cool surface. This one lights up in teal, and while I don't hear anything, only a moment passes before the green doors open and give way to a wide, tall lift. The size is so absurd that I stare at it for a moment before remembering just how huge Oratus are.

"Makes me feel small," Viera says as we get in.

"That's why you're carrying the miners," I reply.

I'd given Viera my miner too, seeing as my shooting is as likely to snipe one of us as it is the enemy. Instead, I followed Malo's choice and grabbed a pair of long, thick tools to wield.

One, a half-meter long bar that ends in a near-point, comes with a strap that lets it rest on my shoulder. The other, a shorter and thicker club with a mallet head, finds an easy grip in my left hand. With either, I should be able to make some useful contribution to a fight without risking too much damage to my friends. The club, after all, is similar to the kukris. A little longer, a little heavier.

Malo does the honors and taps the button to send us down and the lift obeys with a whoosh.

Unlike the lifts on a Vincere ship, or even on the Sevora's moon-smashed Vimelia, this one isn't an austere box of metal. Rather, the side walls shift between static scenes as we move. When we entered the lift, I saw an icy sky with falling, glittering snow catching light from a distant star. Now we're descending surrounded by spinning asteroids in deep space, with splashes of purples and reds scattered around us.

The Amigga are capable of terrible things, but beautiful ones too. Just like humans.

When the lift doors open, though, there's not much of that beauty before us. Instead, the ghost-blue from terminal screens dominates a dark space. Any overhead lights are off, and the only things I can see from the doors are those screens, and the larger, shimmering projections occupying spaces between them.

There are depictions of creatures I've never seen before—things with a multitude of legs, others that appear to be blobs of gas with only a single, small ball floating in the center. Others show carved up landscapes, ridged canyons or a vast, vine-covered plain. All in that white-blue, and all floating just below the height of my eyes.

"Hold up," Malo whispers, again leading the way. "We're not alone."

"I thought they ordered an evacuation," Viera mutters. "Why are people still here?"

"Maybe they're crazy," I say. "Like us."

What Malo sees comes clear to me as I step around a giant, spinning projection of a planet. Clustered farther into the level, messing with a series of images, is an Amigga, along with a trio of Flaum. None of these, though, are carrying weapons. None are wearing armor, though the Amigga appears to float on a microjet machine like the one Ferrolite uses.

"So Ferrolite wasn't lying," the Amigga says, and its low, gravel voice echoes from speakers around us, apparently embedded throughout the level. "The humans really have come home."

With Viera keeping her miners trained on the Flaum and their spherical master, I take the lead, weaving through the projections and the terminals producing them. White spots on the floor bear a faint, deep blue outline, allowing me to see where you might be able to create a chair. One of the Flaum already has a small pedestal next to it, where a device that looks like a Cache is resting.

The aliens watch me, silent and still. I feel like I'm some mythical creature, walking out of legends—or at least, old data logs—to appear in front of disbelievers. Still, unlike the Amigga in the storeroom above, this one lets me speak first.

"We want to know where we came from, and why," I say. "Can you tell us?"

"I don't think you'd believe me if I did," the Amigga replies. "You're not working with that force attacking the bottom of our beautiful tower, are you?"

"Not yet." Technically, we haven't done anything to help Bas and her invaders, and I'm not afraid to take advantage of blurred lines. "We came here to pledge our species to the Chorus, and I want to know why you saw fit to create us."

"Then I will make a deal with you," the Amigga replies. "Put down your miners and let my associates go free. They should leave the Meridia anyway, and I promise you they will not find any guards. Do so, and I will use my access to show you the restricted records that hold your true history."

Trusting an Amigga is like throwing a black-glass knife into the air and trying to catch it; you're going to get hurt. Still, I don't think Viera can shoot us out of this situation. Given our lackluster luck with the terminal in the safe room, getting through without whatever access the Amigga's talking about doesn't seem likely. So while the six eyes of the Flaum trio and the expressionless blob of gray that is the Amigga stares back at me, I have to choose: risk our lives for a chance to see our history?

"Do it," Malo says, and his voice is closer than I expected. I feel him come up behind me, then move next and past me, towards our hostages. "Send the Flaum away. Open the logs."

"Malo? What?"

Malo doesn't glance back at me, but instead points with his toolbar across the level, through the projections and towards the opposite lift. "Go." The Flaum, though, only move when I give the nod and Viera lowers her miners by the smallest of margins. Only when the furry creatures have started their exit does Malo throw an eye my way. "We broke out of that room because you wanted to learn where we came from. If you don't get the chance to see it, then what's the point?"

"You don't sound like you want to know?" I ask Malo, and note that Viera's staying back and out of this argument. T'Oli, too, is sliming away from me and following the Flaum, content to leave its pattered opinions out.

"I know where I come from," Malo replies. "My parents lived in Damantum, though I guess they don't any longer. I'm a Charre warrior, and I serve the Empress and follow the god of all things, Ignos. Nothing else matters."

The Amigga floats there, content to let us argue. Maybe it's studying our behavior, logging our every word into the Chorus' short history of the human race.

"You weren't there," I say to Malo. "When we went back and saw what was left behind, what survived when the Chorus tried to obliterate every bit of us. We were *made*, Malo. Designed and grown. What I don't know is why."

Malo steps back from the Amigga and the terminal behind it. Waves for me to take his place. "Then learn. But Kaishi? Don't tell me. I don't care. I prefer the history I know. Our history."

The warrior can make his own choices, so I take up his offer and walk near the Amigga, who rotates around to face the terminal. It's a large one, with a trio of wide screens, each with a nub on the top that projects blue light onto a platform behind the whole setup. Right now it's showing a landscape, but with a quick buzz-whirr, the Amigga issues some command that slides several pieces out of its floating disk. The tendrils with shiny, short cylinders on the end float towards the ground for a half-moment, then snap towards the terminal and latch onto matching circles.

"We'll secure the area," Viera offers from behind me, as much, I suspect, to give Malo something to do as to hole up from a threat. We all know the Chorus could wipe us out if they cared enough. "You let us know when you're done."

"I'll be fast." It's a promise I can't keep, because I have no idea of the journey I'm about to start, but it seems like the right thing to say.

"Human," the Amigga says. "The curse of my species is that we do not care overmuch for the feelings of others, but I must agree with your friend. What you will see here will expose your past as something better left forgotten. These secrets will not win your war, nor save your kind."

"You don't know that."

The projection behind the terminal shifts as text begins to fill across the screen. Behind and beyond me, I can hear Viera and Malo start moving furniture. Blocking the lifts. Buying me time to learn, and to understand.

"Very well. Your story, such as it is, begins with an accident."

The Amigga's terminal blurs and shifts until I'm seeing another world on its screen. Behind the terminal, the blue projection changes too; into a world I recognize as my own. Earth's continents sit on the slowly-spinning globe, until they're joined by a much smaller oval, one that the projection targets and zooms in on. The terminal joins in, locking into someone's perspective. There's a manicured white-metal hallway, a few Flaum standing by holding all manner of devices and watching as whomever guides the terminal's view glides along.

Glides.

"These are an Amigga's eyes?" I ask.

"In a manner of speaking," the Amigga replies. "This device records and transmits what we might see if we had eyes. We bind our nerves to its receptors, and in doing, gain control over its abilities just as you have over your own limbs."

"Then who is this?"

"Your creator."

Our 'creator' presses on until it gets to a large, circular hatchway. It issues some even-tempered commands to other Flaum—these all wearing full masks, the sheen of them keeping the Flaum's fur pressed down—and the hatch opens. I recognize a shuttle on the other side, and soon enough our guide is in its cockpit.

"What're you going to call this planet?" One of the Flaum pilots asks. "It's not on the registries."

"I haven't thought about it." The guide holds silent for a moment. "We'll choose later on. When we know what's going to happen here."

The recording freezes. I glance up at the projection and its frozen too.

"This is the first inkling we have of Ignos's doubt," the Amigga says to me. "An Amigga should be more confident. We gave Ignos one of the most valuable remaining planets in the galaxy. Ignos told us it would create our last species, and it lied."

"You trusted Ignos, you mean."

"The Amigga don't trust lightly. Reputations are built and maintained, and Ignos had a spotless one. It helped design the Oratus, including the mirrored variant you see all over this tower," the Amigga almost sounds sad here. "So much promise wasted on a flawed premise."

"Which was?"

"That we could create something better than ourselves."

The terminal jolts into another clip before I can investigate that statement. We're in a forest now, one far different from the jungle I grew up in and more resembling those scattered sets up in the Lunare mountains; pines and bits of snow. A brown floor rather than one crawling with ferns. Yet it's verdant all the same, though the view pans through a wide array of Flaum wielding tools or driving massive, lumbering machines tearing their way through the landscape.

"We will need to dig deep," Ignos says to something we cannot see.

"Deep?" the light voice betrays another Flaum.

"Enough to bury our mistakes, and preserve our successes."

The screen shifts again and we're further along. A small brook runs along between a set of trees and a trio of creatures occupies the center, staring at the moving water. The creatures are small, shorter than me, and wear various skin tones, from brown to black and white. Some have tufts of hair sticking out from odd places, like their knees or the middle of their backs. Their hands, too, are shrunken and end in hooked claws.

"Touch it. The water will not harm you," Ignos says.

The creatures hesitate. One casts a look back at the screen, and I see that its left eye takes up nearly half its face, its pupil huge the eyelid a sagging mess. The others, though, look more normal. More human. Yet none of them move to obey the command.

"Touch it, now." The exasperation is obvious in Ignos' voice.

Still, none of them move. A different one opens its mouth, and a low, distorted chirping comes out, like a Flaum's skittering squeak mixed with the hooting calls of an owl. None of them touch the water.

"Too afraid. Increase the aggression and the curiosity in the next batch," Ignos says. "And, please, clean up the hair. They must be adaptable, and hair adds too many complications."

"Anything more with these?" I can't see what asks this question, but it sounds like another Flaum.

"No. Dispose of them."

I blink. Keep myself from stepping back from the terminal. "Ignos just had them killed?"

"A project like this will have numerous failures on the way to success," the Amigga tells me. "Would you rather they were left to roam an unfamiliar world until some predator consumed them? Or, depending on the development stage, they may not have had the ability to eat. To speak or digest. Creating a new species is a messy business."

I'm starting to understand why the Amigga treat everyone as secondary, as tools to be used. If you'd disposed of countless iterations as nothing more than mistakes on the way to your preferred creation, you might not care all that much either.

The terminal flashes again and now we're underground. A space I recognize, though the lack of junk and presence of functioning lights give it a different feel than when I explored the ruined base. Ignos appears to be floating in front of a wall-sized terminal, looking at a lot of different graphs and numbers.

"There's been another conflict," a Flaum's voice, I think the same one from before. "That makes three this week."

"I thought we'd tuned the violence? They passed the tests."

"It's not the violence, Ignos. It's the intelligence. When we made the Oratus, we made them obedient to a fault. These humans, they have too much independence. When they get frustrated, they do not listen. They fight."

"But they can be taught?"

"Yes." The Flaum's voice gets more hopeful. "Our evaluations show, too, that the Sevora will not be able to establish full control."

"Because of that independence."

"Yes. It seems the same will that drives these humans to act in their own interests can allow them to overpower a Sevora's blocks."

"Then we will find another way to calm them down."

The terminal pauses again.

"Do you see the problem?" the Amigga says to me. "Ignos

believed willpower was the key to defeating the Sevora. What it failed to realize was that same willpower could, one day, be used against the Chorus. When we saw these recordings, when we saw Ignos' continued failure to make humans happy in a controlled, defined existence like the Oratus have within the Vincere, we made the choice to end your species before it could proliferate."

"You didn't like that we thought for ourselves?"

"Not only that you thought for yourselves, but that you acted on those impulses. Ignos also had your breeding rate tuned high enough to make galaxy-wide populations a strong possibility. Oratus are controlled. Vyphen, Teven, most species have low enough birth rates to keep them manageable. Flaum are too skittish and ill-equipped for command to be a threat. Humans, though? They would be a problem." The Amigga gives a monotone laugh. "You *are* a problem."

The terminal flashes again, and now Ignos is floating fast towards the base's large docking bay. Things are shaking, panels on the roof are falling in, and the Flaum around Ignos are yelling at each other and the Amigga.

"Make sure the back-up supplies are ready!" Ignos shouts as the Amigga enters the shuttle-filled bay.

When I was last there, the exit had been buried shut. T'Oli, using a stolen shuttle, crashed through the roof to give us a way out. Now, through Ignos' eyes, I can see a wide open ramp leading to bright blue sky. Grass and trees peek around the sides as Ignos takes what looks like a longing glance at an Earth it's about to leave.

"They are. We already have enough stored away." The same Flaum's voice. "Ignos, we have to leave now. The Vincere are sending shuttles down."

"Then we have one chance," Ignos says. "Set the save-state protocol. Make them lose too much, and they might leave us alone."

Ignos floats its way up a shuttle's ramp, and within moments the craft blasts out through the bay. Instead of rising into the sky, however, I watch through Ignos' 'eyes' as the ship barrels through the tops of trees and narrow passes, hugging the ground.

"Chorus, when you see this, know that I don't hold your shortsighted faults against you," Ignos says, and the recording blinks to black. "You may think I have failed, but I promise you, I have not."

"That's the end of it," the Amigga says a second later. "After that transmission, we heard nothing more from Ignos. We commenced a cleansing bombardment of that side of Earth a short time after, and it was assumed Ignos perished in that assault. Now, though, it seems more likely Ignos and its associates died a more natural death after helping your species start again."

So it's all true, then. I'm surprised at myself for the confusion I'm feeling, the disappointment. I guess I had hoped, somehow, that everything I'd suspected was all wrong. That the humans Viera and I discovered on the far side of Earth were a product of some later experiment gone awry, not the original tests for what became Father, Mother, and me. That most of humanity worships the great yellow star in our sky as Ignos makes more sense now—the haunting ghost of where we began.

The unsettled twinges in my gut curdle to distaste. Being the creation of a hard-driving, brutal Amigga isn't a history I want to have. It's not an inspiring story. Not one of overcoming hardship, or creating a better world. It's one alien's idea that, through luck and some planning, survived forced extinction from the rest of the civilized galaxy.

More than all of that, though, I don't want to be the property of the Chorus. I don't want to be their creation. Their *product.*

"Delete it all," I say, and when the Amigga doesn't immediately move to follow my order, I raise the hammer in my right hand. "Do it, now."

"Human, these are sealed records," the Amigga replies. "They are not on Caches. They do not exist anywhere but here, where only those with proper clearance can view them. Humanity's origins will remain a secret, I assure you."

"Yes, they will," I say. "Because you're going to destroy them. Now."

The Amigga hesitates. I gather the creature takes the destruction of knowledge like this as some sort of sacrilege, given the setting and its ability to access these secret records. I, though, see these recordings as evidence of something that doesn't matter.

Before I saw what Ignos did, I believed we came from the dust, from the magic of a god. All of the humans back on Earth believe something similar. Myths and legends, stories are told every day and night about the wondrous ways our civilization grew. These . . . these are nothing. A bad story told by a bad species, and one that doesn't deserve a second telling.

"Do what she asks." Malo appears next to me, and together we use our weapons to imply the consequences.

The threat can't have much weight, as I don't know how the terminals work. How the Chorus stores these recordings. If the Amigga doesn't obey, I don't think we'll be able to—

The terminal flashes. A black circle, outlined in red, appears in the center of the screen. Slowly, the solid red fills in from the outside until the entire circle is complete. Then, with a tiny chime so low I can barely hear it, the terminal goes back to its static, icon-covered screen.

"It's done," the Amigga says. "Your secrets are lost, now."

"How can we trust you?" I ask.

"I do not think I can convince you," the Amigga replies. "You would not understand how to verify. What you can do, though, is choose to believe."

"Choose to believe? That doesn't mean anything."

"Doesn't it? Aren't you making the same argument for your own people? Letting them choose to believe their own stories for their origins?"

I stand with that for a breath. The Amigga's right on all counts, though the thought annoys me. Still, the creature did say that these secrets are only stored here. Why take any chances?

"Malo, let's break these things, and then go find the others. Viera, keep an eye on this one."

The Amigga's smart enough to back away as we start swinging. It doesn't say a word as I bash in one terminal screen after another. As Malo tears apart the thick cords linking things together, prompting sparks to fly in the dark spaces of the level. Despite the size of the place, with both of us working together, we manage to devastate everything fast. I'm sweaty, but smiling at the end of it.

"Feels good getting back to what we know, doesn't it?" Malo says to me when we're done.

"I'm definitely better at smashing these things than using them." I look over at the Amigga, floating silent amid the rubble. "Thank you for your help. When the Chorus falls apart, I'll let whatever replaces them know you're worth keeping around."

"It doesn't matter who's in charge," the Amigga replies as we head towards the lifts. "The cycle's always the same. The stories are forgotten, and then retold."

"What a boring philosophy," Viera mutters. "I think you made the slimeball a little sad."

"It'll get over it." The lift panel, for the one we didn't barricade, sits in front of me. "I'm guessing we need to keep going down?"

T'Oli slithers its way onto my shoulders. "If you want to find those fighters, that's probably a good idea. Unfortunately, these lifts only go back up."

"Then I guess that's where we're heading." I put my hand out, touch Malo's shoulder. "You ready?"

"I am, Empress."

"Viera?"

"I'm ready to shoot something, Kaishi. Let's get'em."

A battle-cry for the ages, I think.

14 / TRAPS AND TRIGGERS

Rovel sputters protests as Sax drags the old Oratus back towards the lift bank. The words aren't worth paying attention to; gibbering insults and petty threats from a coward. Sax has heard the same many times before, usually from his soon-to-be victims.

Not that Sax plans to kill Rovel. No, if there's anything that will serve to turn the Vincere to the side of the Resistance, it's the sight of this creature. This anathema to what an Oratus should be. If the Chorus are willing to do this to an Oratus, then there are no limits to their evils.

"Activate it." Sax pulls Rovel the rest of the way.

"You think I would still be here if they let me use the lifts?" Rovel switches tactics.

It doesn't work.

"Yes." Sax takes Rovel's last remaining claw and presses it against the panel.

As expected, as Sax knew it would even as he hoped, in some small corner of himself, that Rovel really wasn't such a servant of the Amigga, the panel turns green. The nearest lift ought to be coming now, and if Sax is lucky, it'll be the one he's looking for.

"I tried," Rovel says low and soft, defeated. "I told them I would try to turn you, when their methods failed."

"A stupid idea," Sax says.

"Almost as stupid as attacking the Chorus."

Rovel's hiss dies as the lift's doors open, revealing not an empty container that Sax could ride to the top of the Meridia but an Amigga. Or a warbot. Or both. Sax back-steps from the lift while Rovel moves to the side, giving plenty of room for the new arrival to plod out on its trio of metal legs. Those three limbs form the foundation of an exoskeleton that sweeps up and around the gray-green bulk of the Amigga, which is covered in a filmy seal that Sax recognizes as a mask. Splitting the mask are a quartet of metal braces that slide up and over the Amigga like a cage, only this cage has lethal attachments.

Unlike the warbots, which played their weapons off of thin metal limbs streaking from their floating bulks, the Amigga's artillery spreads out over its head like a canopy, with a central beam rising like a rotor sitting across the top of the cage and splaying forth glowing ends like a leaf spreads its veins.

Sax looks at this assembly, at its lethality, and does what any Oratus greeted with such a display would do.

He laughs.

The hissing sound gets the Amigga to freeze, its body settling on those three legs with a creaking halt. The miners over its head angle their points towards Sax, as if that's going to scare him. These Amigga keep forgetting that Sax is supposed to be dead—there's not much to be afraid of when every breath is already borrowed.

"Not the reaction I was expecting," the Amigga says, its voice low and grave, and still monotone. As if a computer were attempting to intimidate Sax. "I suspect you will change your assessment soon enough."

"Not likely."

"Those warbots below are old. Artifacts. Too many Amigga believe we need to rely on others to do our fighting for us," the

Amigga says. "Using those old warbots as a guide, I've designed a way we Amigga can finally take control of our own destinies."

While the Amigga prattles on—Sax suspects the words are more for whomever is watching than Sax himself—he sidesteps towards the left wall of the level. Unfortunately, Rovel hasn't outfitted his floor with anything resembling furniture, so there's no cover on the flat, plain tiles. Without something to hide behind, the best move is going to be a fast assault. And not from where the Amigga expects it.

"You had control of your own destinies," Sax hisses back at the Amigga once its speech breaks, continuing to move. "Look at Rovel. You took him and turned the next version into me, and now you've lost."

"No, we've learned."

The Amigga swivels its body and Sax realizes a second too late that those three legs are designed to go in any direction, and the Amigga can wheel itself in whatever way it chooses. As that array of lasers turns towards Sax, the Oratus jumps towards the level's left wall. Catches on it with his claws, digs in and moves fast, clawing and climbing his way up the side towards the ceiling. Behind him, Sax feels the heat and sees the flashes as the Amigga burns a lot of bolts into the wall beneath him.

When Sax gets to the ceiling, he starts towards the Amigga and stops when a cascade of hot red fire burns in waves directly in front of Sax. The bolts leave a black line scored into the ceiling, and as the whine fades, it's replaced by Rovel's rasping laugh. Sax, frozen, has no doubt the Amigga could have roasted him right there. The monsters array is focused right at Sax, but the Amigga doesn't fire.

"See? This is as easy as it gets," the Amigga says. "Not even an Oratus that has defeated your execution plans can handle my design! After I finish him, give me the seat I deserve!"

There it is. Sax's last question is answered. The lifts stopped here, Rovel's been waiting here, and Sax would bet the warbots were activated all to lead him this way. Survive this far and he'd make a worthy kill for an Amigga looking to elevate itself all the way up to the Chorus.

Sax has been used his entire life. First by the Vincere, and now by Evva. Not once has it made him angry, not until now.

The Oratus drops from the ceiling, pushing off with his claws to fall too fast for the Amigga's array, which starts blinding the level with laser fire, to track Sax. With a twist in mid-air, using the push-off as momentum, Sax hits the ground claws-first and, ignoring the shock of impact-pain, he pushes off towards the Amigga. Sax keeps his body as low to the ground as he can, his vents pressing against the floor as his claws, talons, and tail push him forward.

To its credit, the Amigga isn't so confident in itself that it doesn't try to back up. Those three legs start their rise and fall while the array orients on Sax's charge. Unlike a microjet, though, there's no instant propulsion here. A sacrifice of speed for stability, for the heavy weight arms like the ones the Amigga's carrying require.

Unfortunately, Sax is fast.

The Amigga scores a couple of glancing shots far down Sax's back as the Oratus leaps, the pain washed away by Sax's bloodlust—that unquenchable thirst for the destruction of everything lying between Sax and his goals. The Oratus hits the Amigga in the middle, and Sax drives his claws through the mask's main weakness: close, personal, devastating blows. Every part of Sax contributes—his mouth tearing away the array's attachment to the rest of the Amigga, his claws shredding apart the cage and the creature inside of it, his talons ripping away the connections to those thick legs. Sax's tail, too, gets in a good whack when Rovel makes a worthless attempt to dislodge Sax from the assault, sending the old Oratus crumpling back against the very water station Rovel sat next to when Sax first arrived on this level.

Before the Amigga can say another word, before it can fire another shot, it's gone, and Sax is gulping down the remnants. He's never actually eaten an Amigga before, and while few things compare with the delicious, furry meat of a Flaum, Sax doesn't mind the mid-mission snack.

With sparking remnants littering the floor around him, Sax rises from the kill and turns back to Rovel, who's fallen into pure groveling mode now that his apparent benefactor's met the fate Rovel deserved cycles ago.

"Please," Rovel says, his voice a sickening whine. "I had no choice."

Sax doesn't answer. There's one thing he still needs from Rovel, and he understands that the only thing this Oratus truly values is its own skin. A currency as easy to exploit as any other.

"Then let me give you one," Sax replies, pouring every bit of a real Oratus' hiss into the words. "You will get me to the top of the Meridia, or I will give you your death here and now."

"The top?" Rovel says, and here his eyes track to the other lift panel, opposite where the Amigga came from. "I don't have that clearance. Allocite, the Amigga you just . . . ate, would have been able to take you there."

"Then how close?" Sax says.

Rovel pauses, again throwing eyes towards the other bank of lifts, then the Oratus gets back on its talons. "Close enough, I think, for you to go the rest of the way."

At a wave from Sax's foreclaw, Rovel leads the way to those lifts and places his claw on the control panel. Once again, it turns green. This time, though, a lift doesn't immediately open, and a series of numbers appears on the panel.

"A queue," Rovel explains when Sax gives a slight warning hiss. "No games. There aren't many lifts that can traverse so many levels. For security, I believe. I don't have a priority clearance."

Sax can agree with the Chorus on one thing—trusting Rovel with anything important would be a mistake.

"After I leave," Sax says. "Summon another lift and go down. Find Evva and tell her what you did."

"They'll kill me if I do."

"I'll kill you if you don't," Sax puts a single foreclaw against Rovel's nose. "You turned against your own species. I can't say what the galaxy will look like when the Chorus falls, but perhaps, if you help us get through this tower, there might be a place in it for you."

The traitor's access might not last long once whichever Amigga controls such things realizes Rovel isn't on their side anymore, but even if the Oratus' claws get the fighters up a few more levels, then it's worth the attempt.

"I didn't want to do it," Rovel tries again as the counter on the panel ticks lower. "You see these stumps? They were burned off. One by one. Allocite made me fight, made me try to destroy its tests."

"You failed."

It's the truth, and it's devastating. Rovel shrinks away from Sax, goes back to the wall and sits, staring sullen towards his fellow Oratus. For his part, Sax is just fine cutting off the conversation. The stakes have been laid, the deal's been made, and there's no reason anymore to suffer the conversation of someone so lost as Rovel. Maybe Evva can redeem the old one, if she cares to try.

The lift dings a moment later, arrives empty, and Sax delivers one more hard stare to Rovel. A look that ought to haunt the Oratus' nightmares. One more price for him to pay, and far from enough.

A coward.

Sax would die a thousand times first.

15 / PROMISES

Despite being armed and ready for anything, my twitchy aggression, spiked after our successful destruction of my own species' history, falters when I'm confronted with what's pasted in gold-rimmed Chorus blue on each of the lift's three walls and, once they close, the two doors:

RESEARCH AND ARCHIVES ONLY

As if to confirm the words, the panel only lists ten levels, each of which is higher than the one we're just leaving. Their labels are vague enough to be interesting—one level reads out *Planets and Planetoids* while another discusses *Robotics and Mechanical Recovery.* None of them, though, seem like they'll take us to Bas and the other fighters.

"Where do you think we should go?" I ask. There's a brief silence, and then the quiet patters give truth to my suspicions: T'Oli has an opinion.

"This is a dedicated lift, and I would assume most levels have lifts like this," the Ooblot says. "Given that we're likely to be pursued, and that the Chorus will know where we are the moment we leave this lift, I suggest we choose the level that sounds like the most fun."

"The puddle's got a point," Viera says. "Let's go there." The

Lunare points to the sixth one above ours, a level titled *Astronavigation and the Vincere.* "Figure, if nothing else, we can get a glimpse of what kind of weapons we'll be up against when the Vincere comes after Earth."

"You and I both know they'll blow us up from orbit." Nonetheless, I press the button. "If the Chorus doesn't die here, humans are probably done."

"They may not hold the rest of your species responsible for your crimes," T'Oli says as the lift churns to life, whisking us upward. "Humanity may yet have a chance to enslave themselves to the Chorus' will."

"Is the Ooblot always this way?" Malo asks, and Viera and I give him our exhausted affirmatives at the same time.

"We are, always, who we are," T'Oli responds.

The lift doors, thankfully, put an end to that conversation with a smooth opening. Beyond them is a level that, at first, seems similar to the one we just left. Terminals abound, and blue projections fill in most of the gaps in the dark room. Instead of landscapes, of worlds and recordings, these are floating images of ships and whole fleets. In the very center, surrounded by terminals, and down a slight ramp into the space, swirls what looks like a grid of glowing stars.

"See anyone?" I say as we step out of the lift.

My eyes aren't picking up anything, though some terminals show things in the midst of being run—one has a recording going of some battle, another is showing the continued feed from the assault below. A couple containers of nutrient goop sit half-eaten on a small table made of the same white stuff that ought to have descended back to the floor after its use.

"Looks like they were interrupted," Viera says, coming up the center with me.

"By the evacuation." Malo breaks right, stepping around a slow-spinning image of a three-pronged ship that looks like it holds a single pilot.

"Or us," I say. "If T'Oli's right, everyone saw what we were doing down there."

"And they chose not to stop us?"

"They may have other priorities," T'Oli says from my shoulders. "A small group of humans, easily defeated, may not be worth the attention of the guards at this time."

I get to the center and notice that grid of stars isn't just a nameless work of art. Instead, each one of the pulsing spheres has a name, and when I reach out with my hand to touch the nearest one, it flashes and rises above the others. Then it floats to the middle of the grid, before, like an egg opening from the top, spreading apart and sending out countless little images. At first I'm not sure what I'm looking at, but then the blue light resolves the blurs into tiny ships, many clustered together. Like a formation.

"Fleets," I say when the word makes its way through my awed mind. "This, this must be every Vincere force in the galaxy."

I look down at the names again, hunting for one in particular. It's not far from the one I grabbed at random—Kolas. I touch the sphere for the Oratus' fleet, and the one I'd opened retracts and slides back to its place in the grid. Kolas' ships blow into the space, and I note too that the word 'Aspicis' sits above the mix of craft. So the Chorus has the size and location of their fleets available in an instant to any of them. Back in Damantum, it would have been so useful to know where my generals were, what my hunters were doing or who was still alive after a far away battle.

"Wake up, Empress." Viera's tone is tight. "Incoming."

From the lift behind us, next to the one we came in, a set of six Flaum emerge with their miners holstered and their mouths agape. Which, seeing as I'm a classified species standing in the middle of dozens of floating ships, makes some sort of sense.

"Hi," I say to them as they shuffle out of the lift. To my right, Viera's hunkered down behind the terminals, the lowered central area giving her just enough cover. Malo's found a place to hide to my left. T'Oli's wrapped itself around my chest, but its eyestalks are hidden behind my head. All in all, we're pretty well set for an ambush. "Can I help you?"

One Flaum feels brave enough to take the lead and steps in front of its friends, closer to me. This one has deep brown fur, pocked with patches of white. It would be pretty if not for the blue, over-sized Chorus vest hanging over its shoulders. Apparently it thinks I'm harmless because neither of its claws go for weapons.

"Who are you?" the Flaum's voice is scratchy, high.

"Kaishi," I say. If they don't know who I am, then my name has to be meaningless. All I'm angling for now is a trip to that lift they came in on. If we can get there without getting us killed, well, I'll take it. "Human ambassador to the Chorus."

The Flaum sniffs. Cocks its head. "Human?"

Our stimulating conversation is cut short before I can reply. Through the ever-present intercoms, a voice I recognize in its bland monotony comes through loud and clear.

"These are the ones I ordered you to find!" Ferrolite's command pours out around us. "Take them, and bring them to my shuttle."

The Flaum all jerk, like puppets on strings, at Ferrolite's command. The lead one, with the patched fur, is the only one that doesn't reach for its miner. Instead, its eyes widen at me as its mouth opens to ask the obvious question, "Will you come with us?"

If we go with those Flaum and get on Ferrolite's shuttle, we're dead. As it is, we're likely dead anyway, but I'd rather die fighting. I hope Viera and Malo agree with me, cause they're about to lose their options.

"Nah," I say. "I've got better things to do."

For a second I wonder if the Flaum's going to ask *"what things?"* but Viera doesn't give the creature the time to respond. She pops up from behind the terminal and lets loose with both miners. I'm surprised to see blue bolts lance out from the weapons and wonder if Viera's grown a conscience.

I feel T'Oli forming up its usual sword onto my right hand. I shift the hooked bar tool to my left and take a running step through the blue lights of Kolas' fleet towards the Flaum.

And don't make it more than a stride. Malo gets there first, as the Flaum yanks a miner from its holster and aims it at me. My warrior slams his metal bar onto the Flaum, cracking its head and sending the creature crumpling to the ground. Behind it, the other furry Chorus forces dive and duck behind terminals, some sending back a shot or two our way. The lift they came in, too, snaps shut.

"We have to get out of here," T'Oli patters to me. "They'll have reinforcements coming."

"Way ahead of you." For once, I actually am. Seeing Malo down the Flaum has me reversing course, turning and heading to the level's opposite side, where another pair of lifts glow beyond more terminals and floating depictions of ships and stars. "C'mon! To the other side!"

"I'll cover you!" Viera shouts. "Go!"

I'm already moving. In the past, maybe, I'd have panicked at the idea of leaving Viera behind, but now I know what matters is getting to those lifts. Getting them open. Then we'll find a way to keep the Flaum off the Lunare till she gets over to us. So instead I run and jump, dive and duck my way towards the far side as an increasing number of blue bolts flash around me. The Flaum are getting braver, but they're losing the accuracy battle as I get further and further away.

The lift on the left is like the one we took here—pasted over with a dedicated level warning, because the Chorus value their scientists enough for two dedicated lifts. The lift on the right, though, is the same all clear gray like the first one we rode. I slap at the panel to summon the lift, then drop as a pair of shots slam into the wall above me. I'm not on the ground for more than a breath before Malo slides along next to me.

"Made it," he says, and I notice he's added the Flaum's miner to his mask. "You all right?"

"Still breathing. Viera?"

"Still shooting."

I nod towards the lift. "It's coming."

Malo jerks around the terminal for a quick look, raises the miner and squeezes off a shot. There's a sharp squeal back in the dark.

"Viera!" Malo shouts. "Go now! I have you covered!"

"Easy to say!" Viera calls back.

I, without a miner or a good way to see what's happening, sit with my legs bunched, ready to spring as soon as the lift's doors open. It's frustrating that I can't shoot, that I can't swing, but I suppose that's the job of an Empress; depend on those you trust to make your plans succeed.

The lift dings, the panel turns green. Malo's still looking back towards Viera, still shooting into the dark when the doors swing open. When I see something that makes my jump, my rapid scramble for our escape die before it ever starts; a mirrored Oratus.

It's easier to see in the dim light here than the washed-out white and reds in the Chorus chambers. Here, the Oratus' scales don't quite know how to reflect the blues and black, and as a result there's a hazy teal cast to the creature that lets me see its wicked teeth in all their glory as its head turns towards Malo and I.

"Kaishi," T'Oli says. "You can't beat this creature."

The Ooblot's talking like that because, in spite of the fear twisting and tying me in knots, I'm standing up. I'm stepping around Malo, who's just noticing what's come to find us, and I'm staring the beast full on.

"Don't tell a human what she can't do," I mutter to the Ooblot. The Oratus gets its giant self out of the lift, all three meters and more, and glares down at me. "Give me my sword, T'Oli. I'm gonna need it."

The Ooblot, at least, doesn't ask questions when I give it a command. Its cream self, blotched now because of shots taken and scars earned on our journeys, grants me my razor's edge, extending out from my hand half a meter. Sharp, deadly, and completely inadequate to the task at hand.

"Give up, human," the mirrored Oratus hisses. "You cannot win. Your species is not designed for it."

"Getting real tired of people insulting my species." I step forward with my left, stab in with my right and send T'Oli's point rocketing in towards the bottom half of the Oratus' torso.

If there's one hope I have in here, it's that all the terminals create tight quarters for a creature as big as the Oratus. It's going to have a hard time dodging, jumping, or doing much of anything with its tail. So the Oratus does something stupid and tries to grab my strike. T'Oli does some lightning work and reforms itself as we slash, coating my wrist in its nigh-invincible skin and narrowing its blade to a needle's point. The mirrored Oratus' left midclaw closes on my wrist and its claws slide off my new armor, allowing my strike to slip past and deliver a solid stab.

The only reaction as T'Oli gets a puncture's view of an Oratus' insides is a hissing snarl, and then the thing's left foreclaw backhands me into the wall next to the lifts. It's a hard hit by an arm as tall as I am, and I bounce off the wall and sprawl to the floor, only to find that T'Oli's not on my right hand anymore. I push back, trying to force the cobwebs from my shaken head, and stand up. It takes two seconds for me to do that, which is more time than I should have.

But the Ooblot's saving my life again.

T'Oli's flowing around the mirrored Oratus like the most annoying bug you could imagine. Its Ooblot body slides along the mirrored Oratus' scales, getting just out of the way of the creature's claws or teeth. T'Oli's not just annoying the monster either—I can see bits of its fluid form changing into tiny points and biting, piercing into the Oratus' scales as they move.

"We have to go, Kaishi," Malo's at my side, and he's pushing me towards the open lift door. "Now."

"Can't you shoot it?"

"I tried," Malo replies as we move. "The shot bounced off."

I have a litany of other ideas, but close them off as Malo pushes me into the lift. The mirrored Oratus finally manages to snare one of

T'Oli's two eyestalks and tears the Ooblot off its scaly hide, then flings my friend deep into the level. Those yellow-green Oratus eyes turn towards us next, and I slam the panel inside the lift, commanding the doors to close. And as the Oratus' foreclaws swipe towards us, the Meridia does what we need, and the lift doors slide shut.

There's the brief sound of claws on metal, and then the lift's whisking away. To what level, I don't know.

But my friends won't be there.

16 / THE SMALL GALAXY

Stars.

Thousands. No, millions. More.

The lift opens onto a light-less level brighter than any Sax has been to within the Meridia. Despite the inky walls, the padded black floor and the empty dark ceiling, the galaxy swirling inside this space makes it simple to see. The twinkling stars, the miniature nebulae, and the pulsing core at the center, though, make understanding much harder.

The lift's panel—the only concession to practicality Sax can see on the level—glows red, telling him his current hijacked ride won't be going any further. So Sax walks into the starry swirl. At three meters tall, Sax is used to looking down at things, but here he's in the middle of the lights. Unknown balls of blue and white fire dance by his eyes while clouds of purple and blue slide into and through his scales, appearing on his other side as though Sax means nothing in this level-sized galaxy.

What is this? The question frays Sax's drive, shunting aside the focus on the Priority Beam with a taste of the same wonder Sax felt on *Nova*, watching a star burst with Bas by his side. On that station, the point had been to relax, to marvel at what nature could create.

This hits him in the same way, and Sax almost falls into its spinning spell before a voice speaks out:

"Solis."

At the words, toned in an Amigga's unnatural voice, the galaxy freezes its rotation. Then, with the slightest shiver, the stars and gas clouds blow out around Sax, vanishing into the room's black walls. The push isn't even—the galaxy's center coasts to one side and a different star, at first just the slightest glow, takes center stage. Zooming in.

The Oratus catches what's going on and snaps his eyes from the spectacle. Keeps the two far lifts in view, with a quick snap glance behind him to make sure surprises aren't using the distraction as an opportunity to claim Sax as a victim. But there's no beeps, no whooshing doors. Nothing but Sax alone here with a voice and, now, his home.

"We're evacuating," the voice speaks again and Sax catches it now. The First Chair. "I'm the only one of the Chorus still here."

Solis, a rocky wasteland of a world, spins in front of Sax, and the room itself flushes with yellow light from his homeworld's star, lingering at the very edge of the projection. As Solis spins, the fertile green scar placed there by a species bent on growing another, comes and goes from view. Of the ships orbiting the planet, there is no sign. Not a military tool, then.

"Why are you staying?" Sax hisses to the air. With the lifts locked, his choices are few, and if the First Chair is willing to speak with him, then the least Sax can do is hold the Amigga's attention and keep it away from Bas, Evva, and the rest. "Shouldn't you have been the first one away?"

"The Chorus changes over only in times of crisis," the First Chair says. "I've allowed this pathetic resistance to arise. Responsibility demands I be the one to see to its destruction. If I fail, the Chorus will elect a new First Chair, one who will guide the Vincere in doing what I could not."

"So you're the only one that's not a coward." Sax stalks closer to the planet, leering down towards it. Trying, and succeeding, to pick out those rock arches where he dropped from so long ago.

The First Chair manages a laugh, a jarring series of blips that reminds Sax of a broken alarm. "If I fled, I would be executed for abdicating my duties. I stay because it is my only chance at life. Just like you, fighting when you should be dead."

"If you want to kill me, you'll have to try harder."

"I don't want to kill anyone. At least, I didn't," the First Chair says. Sax finds that hard to believe, but the First Chair drags the end of the phrase into a sigh, suggesting a truth made impossible by reality. "Part of running a civilization is coming to terms with the less savory parts of it. Learning that everyone will not understand or agree with you, and that they will hate you for your choices."

"Because your choices hurt them."

"Yes. Creating the Oratus *did* hurt many of us. Creating you may wind up being the end of our species, if we can't shut down that insurrection going on below." Solis spins away and the galaxy, or at least part of it, reappears.

Sax stands in the middle of a collection of stars. Solis's system hovers to his right, while a clustered band that includes Aspicis dominates the center of the level. The planets are too small to see, but as Sax focuses on any of the stars, the names of the systems appear like mist over the red, blue, white and yellow orbs.

"This is our home," the First Chair continues. "This small part of the galaxy holds most of our intelligent life. Without the Chorus, it would not exist. Even if space-faring technology had fallen into the grasp of every species, they would have torn themselves apart in war without us."

"You don't know that."

"We do," the First Chair delivers this edict with the tired patience of a commander pointing out the obvious. "We've seen it. Stopped the senseless destruction so many times with the honeyed gifts of our miracles. And after that technology was brought against us, we destroyed those who dared and kept only the simplest ones. Only the safest species."

Time is difficult to judge. Cycles, with their indeterminate length, give Sax little idea of how long the Chorus has been in power. The potential span twinges his mind, makes him wonder how arrogant Evva and the rest of them are for attempting something that must have been tried many times before. If the First Chair is speaking truth, then the Chorus has seen many worse rebellions, many more difficult fights.

And yet, Sax is still here. By the First Chair's own words, Evva is progressing. So something must have changed. The Chorus must be weaker. The First Chair is keeping quiet. Content to let Sax work through the implications.

"Then you made us." Sax speaks as the realization comes through. The Oratus are the difference this time. A species so strong, so deadly that the Amigga needed to keep control of them to survive. "We're the problem."

"Like the artificial intelligences we crafted before you, the solution has once again turned on us," the First Chair confirms. "All I can hope for is that we can defeat your friends here, and reduce your species to irrelevance before it happens again."

The galaxy zooms out, expanding until the endless stars once again swirl around the room.

"Why are you telling me this?" Sax hisses. As much as he'd like to keep the First Chair talking, he's fascinated. No enemy ought to reveal its goals to its opponent, not unless victory, or defeat, was assured.

"Because, Oratus. You have a choice to make. Before, I offered you a chance to save your friends. Now, I offer you a chance to save your species."

"But you just—"

"I said irrelevance, not extinction. The Chorus will remove your species from the Vincere. You will be given worlds to control, and like the Vyphen, be allowed to choose your own destinies."

"I'm not the one who can make that choice." A three-letter Oratus deciding the fate of his species? Sax doesn't think Evva would be a fan of that.

"Your friends will not listen to me. They might listen to you," the First Chair says. "Agree, and I'll send a lift to where you can meet them. Discuss the offer, and decide."

The lift Sax arrived in blinks green and its doors open, inviting a clean, Flaum-less interior. The two guards Sax took care of must have survived. Picked themselves off the ground and crawled away to wherever the Chorus stashed the guards who lost. They were—

Irrelevant.

This fight isn't only about survival. Not just about casting the Amigga from the top in a desperate bid avoid elimination, but also to say they deserve a chance at their own destinies. Living under the weight of the Chorus, knowing their charity drew the border for the Oratus' part in the galaxy, would be as bad as a slow, creeping descent into extinction.

Better to swing the claws while he has them. Better to attack the enemy while he can.

"You hesitate." The toneless voice comes through the galaxy, as if the cosmos itself is speaking to Sax.

Behind that voice is no god. Behind that voice is prey.

"Tell the lift to bring me to you," Sax hisses. "Then we can begin a negotiation that matters."

The reply comes by the slamming of the lift doors. The flash of red on the lift panels as the lock, sealing Sax on the level, trapped within the spinning lights.

"So you're a coward, like all of the other Amigga," Sax says, prowling the edges of the room. No idea if the First Chair is even listening, but the words feel good to say.

Sax tests the dark walls with his claws, and while they're soft at first touch—a surface more adept at catching the projection's light without reflecting it in a blinding back-and-forth—beneath is the same hard metals Sax would expect to find on a Vincere ship. With time, Sax could carve his way through. With that same time, Bas, Evva, and the others would all be dead.

The center of the galaxy is the brightest part, a dense cluster of stars in myriad colors pulsing. Sax heads to it next, takes in the lights. Touches the shape with a claw, and when it doesn't react, Sax has to stop himself from getting carried away by philosophical meanderings. Maybe it's being here, at the center of civilization's power, or that he's been alone and on the edge of death so often, but Sax keeps drifting into the sorts of ideas an Oratus isn't meant to have.

Purpose, for a living weapon, shouldn't be hard to define.

The chime of another lift arriving kills the musings, letting Sax turn and settle himself for whatever surprises the First Chair's sent his way.

Sax has never seen a single enemy more than twice. They're either dead, or, well, dead after the second encounter with Sax's biting jaws or razor claws. So when Kah clacks his way out of the lift, followed by a second mirrored Oratus, their reflective scales making the dancing galaxy all the more mesmerizing, Sax gives Kah a star-lit grin.

Time to correct this error.

"Even after all the First Chair's offering you, there's no thought of surrender?" Kah asks as he moves to one side of the galaxy while the other Oratus heads opposite, trapping Sax in the middle.

"So you can use me against my own pair?" Sax hisses. "Those aren't Oratus tactics, Kah. You know better."

"I know you're too headstrong to understand what's right," Kah replies.

The Oratus has plenty of scars from their last tussle in the broadcasting level, and the way Kah sits back on his talons, keeps his fore- and midclaws up makes it clear the Oratus has no desire to tangle with Sax.

Sax is about to fire back, but stops. The two mirrored Oratus haven't attacked him yet, and they're not supported by what should be a crushing amount of armed Flaum. Then there's the First Chair, spending time talking to Sax, trying to get the Oratus to change his mind.

"Two of you?" Sax says instead. "Two of you. In all of the Meridia, that's what you send against an enemy this far up your invincible tower?"

Kah gives a low growl, switches his tail across the floor as stars and nebulae blow through him. The reflective skin mirrors those floating sparks, making Kah appear less invisible and more a distorting curve in the swirl of this miniature universe.

"In moments, the Vincere will sweep down from above and blow apart your pair and your Resistance," Kah says. "You could save them. Tell them to give up."

"So you'd destroy the Meridia to save . . . what, exactly? The Amigga that have already escaped?"

Bluffs. Bluster and threats. It's hard to believe that Sax thought the Chorus a strong and immortal fixture for so long when the illusion of their power is so clear now. All of these species in thrall to their commands because the idea of rebelling seemed so impossible, but when you're actually fighting them . . .

Turns out the Chorus isn't quite so tough.

Kah's opening that mouth, inhaling with those vents, when Sax makes the move. He leaps through the galaxy's burning core at the mirrored Oratus. Standing straight, tall, and ready, Kah would have been able to meet Sax's leap with any number of counters. As he's mid-breath, though, Kah makes a fumbling, tripping retreat back to the galaxy's outer edges, flinging his claws up to deflect Sax's swiping charge.

Sax presses the attack for two seconds. Enough for each of his four claws to get a single rake in, then he uses his momentum to press past Kah, turning to the right and snaking his tail up and over the bracing Kah's shoulders. With a snap, Sax pushes Kah forward, right where Sax was and right where the other mirrored Oratus, rampaging from behind through the blinding clouds of interstellar brilliance, dives.

Mirrored Oratus rely on their stealthy scales to throw their opposition off balance, to make shots fire wide and security systems miss their very presence. As they're all elite servants of the Chorus, Sax figures they haven't spent much time training against each other, learning to recognize their own telltale blurs when targeting a strike.

The hypothesis proves true when Kah meets the slashing swipes and snapping bites of his supposed ally, a flurry of blows that cuts through Kah's already-unraveling defense and re-opens plenty of old wounds.

And by the time the mirrored Oratus realizes its mistake, Kah's reeling away and Sax is making his own attacking leap. Both of Sax's talons catch on the mirrored Oratus' torso, biting to the creature's chest and back, and giving Sax the one moment he needs to make lethal work with his jaws on the enemy's exposed head.

The body rides to the floor, and Sax settles with it, locking eyes with Kah the entire way. The mirrored Oratus looks at what remains of his companion, and lets loose a long sigh from his vents.

"You don't have to," Sax offers, though, with the bloodlust pulsing through him, he wouldn't mind if Kah decides to go down thrashing. "They don't control you."

"No," Kah hisses. "They do not."

There's vulnerability in those words. An opening for one of Bas' verbal snipes. A method of attack Sax would have sneered at not long ago, but that now makes an increasing amount of sense.

"Look at what's around us," Sax says, pointing with his claws at the infinite stars. "You want to give up the chance to see all of this just because some Amigga told you to?"

Kah hisses a dour laugh, runs his claws along his new injuries, as if trying to see if they're as long and bloody as they feel. "If you lose, then the Chorus will kill me and I'll see none of it."

"Do you think we'll lose? After this?"

"I wasn't lying," Kah says. "We've been herding your friends. They're going to find themselves sealed on a pair of levels soon. The Vincere will hit those two with targeted antipersonnel blasts. They'll all die, and the tower will survive."

Only one reason for Kah to tell Sax this: the mirrored Oratus doesn't want them to lose. Or, Kah just wants to get Sax focused on something else to launch some surprise assault, but given that Kah stands still, wounded, and doing nothing with those claws suggests the former.

"How can I stop them?" Sax says.

"You can't," Kah replies. "Only the First Chair could order Nalucite to go back on the plan, and that won't happen."

Sax doesn't know the name, but now he has a new objective. It won't do any good to get to the Priority Beam and send a message if Evva and the others are reduced to charred ash flitting through Aspicis' sky.

"Then help me find this Nalucite," Sax says.

Kah's already moving as Sax says the words. Stepping long and slow past Sax and towards those locked lifts. "Nalucite is the Meridia, Sax. There are other Amigga that help, that keep tabs on isolated systems, but this one? It won't be easy."

"Because it's been easy so far." Sax follows Kah to the lifts and watches as the mirrored Oratus places a foreclaw on the lift panel, which turns that beautiful shade of grass-green.

When the lift's doors open, though, Kah doesn't move towards them. Sax gives the mirrored Oratus a breath, but when Kah only stares his way, Sax gets the hint and goes inside alone.

"Tell it to take you to level zero," Kah says. "That's where you'll find it."

"You're not coming?"

"You just offered me freedom," Kah replies. "I'm going to take you up on it, and get out of here before someone decides I'm better off dead."

Sax barely gets a nod off before the lift doors close. The lift sits still, waiting for Sax to give it a command. Level zero. That sounds like it would be all the way down. A long and steep drop, and the opposite direction from the Priority Beam.

"Zero." Sax says the word.

Anything for Bas.

17 / GOING BACK

Gone. After I swore I wouldn't leave another friend behind, with the shutting of those lift doors I've left two. Viera and T'Oli, ditched on a level full of enemies. The glimmering teeth of that mirrored Oratus, snarling towards us in the blue-dark light, haunt me the entire lift ride, which, thankfully, is short enough for Malo to tell me we'll find them only three times.

"We will," Malo insists again as the lift doors open. "I swear."

I don't answer, because the part of me that thinks of the Ooblot and the Lunare is numb and doesn't want to process anything other than the opening stages of grief. So, when my eyes catch the terrifying display in front of us, I'm grateful for the distraction. Fear is better than loss, curiosity better than sadness.

The rows of floor-to-ceiling tubes in this level bring plenty of fear as they glow, illuminating with the same sapphire lighting scheme this section of the Meridia prefers. The lights are, this time, implanted in the tops of the tubes, and the liquid inside each shifts around as some circulating current keeps things lively. The effect makes the entire level appear under water, shadows playing in the glass forest as I walk into it. Malo comes behind, his metal bar raised and ready.

"I recognize this place," I say mostly to myself. I've seen similar things on Vimelia, on *Cobalt*. These tubes aren't empty—half-formed species linger in each of them, some looking closer to Flaum, while others resemble mossy rocks or stringy, shapeless tendril masses.

"You've been here?" Malo answers anyway.

"No, not exactly," I reply, continuing to go forward. At the base of every tube is a small terminal displaying a simple read-out I actually understand—temperature, pulse, the sorts of rudimentary medical terms we'd even defined in Damantum. "The Cache showed me an entire ship full of these once. A Sevora craft. They were growing new hosts."

"Why would the Chorus have this, then?"

"For the same reason." I head over to a terminal in front of a stone-silent Flaum that looks more or less normal, albeit submerged in water. Beyond the vital signs, I flick my finger through graphs and diagrams, through code names and equations I don't understand. "Only instead of giving them over to parasites, I think these are for experiments."

Malo stares at me and I can see the disgust in his eyes. "Kaishi, why did you pick this level?"

The lifts that I can see, a similar double-bank on either side, have panels glowing a bright red. I don't need to be up close to know that they'll be locked, keeping us on this level. So I lean back against the Flaum's tube, my hands at my sides.

"I didn't choose it," I say. "The lift stopped here on its own."

"But, why?"

"Malo, who cares why?" I want to be frustrated, angry. Despairing and enraged all at once. I want to be in one of these tubes too—lifeless and floating, watching the eons pass without a single concern. "One of the Chorus did it. Or maybe the lift was already going here. They have Viera and T'Oli, and they're going to come for us too. It's over. Done."

Even leaving Vimelia that first time, with Malo gone and out of reach, I didn't feel so lost. Not even on *Cobalt*, as the Amigga poked and tore at me. Or on Earth, as the Sevora launched attack after attack and every human in Marilo knew it was only a matter of days till we died. I can't find a hold here, not in this tower with all its horrors. Not now.

But Malo, my true friend, tries his best. He picks up my sorrow and carries it back to me, putting his arms on and then around my shoulders. Maybe he expects me to cry here, but I can't bring myself to do it. This is too far past grief now; not only are we trapped, but I never finished the oath. As soon as the Chorus deals with Bas' little insurrection, they'll carry my crimes back to Earth and deliver the punishment to my people, to Avril and all the others depending on us for safety. Waiting for the miracles we promised them.

"We can't give up, Kaishi." Malo tries talking. "You didn't give up on me. You came back."

I shake my head against his skin and watch the blue lights play on the far wall, try not to see what's in the tubes lining it. "Malo, we did give up. We were sure you were dead. The only reason we came to Vimelia was because Lan and Kolas brought us there."

Malo's silent, and for a second I wonder if he's going to let go, drop me right here and now. Instead, Malo hugs me tighter. "But when you knew, when you had the choice, you risked everything for me. This is no different. We'll get them back."

There's plenty of differences, and I open my mouth, an angry heat rising to explain to Malo just how different it is to launch a rescue mission with a pair of Oratus, plenty of weapons, and the backing of an entire Vincere fleet compared to a couple of lost humans trapped in a tower full of all-knowing enemies.

I don't, though, say a word.

Because something else speaks instead.

"Why not join them?" Ferrolite's voice, like it did on the other level, echoes out around the tubes. Amused, tinged with static and echoing off the glass, the Amigga's words lend to the ethereal nature of the place. Of my current state of mind.

"You're not killing her," Malo says, stepping back from me, lifting the bar, and searching for the Amigga.

"Of course not," Ferrolite replies. "That would only hurt my reputation. I brought you humans here to bind yourselves to the Chorus, and that will happen. Your friends are alive, and they are waiting for you."

I'm too tired, too warped by the struggles of the day to play word games with the Amigga, so I glare at the ceiling and hope the creature can see my face. "No."

That's it. That's all I'm saying to that thing. Ferrolite did, though, shake me out of the black cloak threatening to suffocate me there on that level. Its cold reasoning brushes away the shroud, and I replace it with fatalistic determination: if we're going to lose, we might as well give it everything we have. So I give Malo a nod.

"Are you ready?" Malo asks me.

"I'm ready."

"Ready for what?" Ferrolite says. "Aren't you going to save your friends?"

We walk back to the lift we came in, the silver one that's supposedly able to traverse most of the Meridia. The red panel's still there, still locked. I try tapping at it, but there's no response. Malo works his bar on the lift doors, but gets nothing more than a few scratches on the smooth surface.

"You have two choices humans," Ferrolite says as I try a more blunt method, banging my bar to no effect. "Either accept my offer, or rot here until someone cares enough to send guards to finish you off."

"I don't think we're getting through here," Malo says to me. "At least, not with force."

"Then let's look around," I reply. "There has to be some way out."

So we commence the search. I look around terminals, press buttons on the ones I can find, and even take a brief detour in the Cache only to find that the Meridia exists as nothing more than a vague notion. The Sevora, apparently, never managed to get a spy in here. I should have exchanged my Cache for a new one on Kolas' ship, but then, looking at the deep emerald bracelet, I'd be leaving a piece of this whole journey behind.

Meridia's levels aren't tiny—each one is only a little smaller than a section on a Sevora seed ship, or almost the size of my own village. Even so, it becomes clear pretty quickly that we're not going to find an exit. All the terminals are secured or confusing, the four lifts refuse to open, and beyond the forest of tubes, there's not a single answer for our problem. Other than the one Ferrolite constantly pushes into our ears.

"You have no other choice!" Ferrolite states, and I'm getting impressed by the sheer number of ways it's demanded we listen to it.

"Why do you care?" I say. "Is your reputation that important to you?"

"It's all we have! The Chorus members are slotted by their contributions to the Amigga species—so I need this. I need your oath. And you need it too, humans. Your species needs our protection, our technology." Ferrolite's tone doesn't change, not quite, but its tactics shift all the same. "Aren't you tired of this? All these strange things, these fights, this destruction. You've already cleansed your past of its unwanted origins. Take your victory and go home."

Malo catches my eye and he does look tired. I'm sure I'm no treat either, coated with sweat from running through this station, tired and sore. The thought of waking up to a cool ocean breeze, watching Ignos—I refuse to combine that terrible Amigga, that terrible Sevora, with the god of my tribe—rise over the horizon . . . maybe it's worth saying yes one more time. I've just been in the deepest despair I've ever felt, and here's a rope to climb out of it.

"You'll let us leave? Unharmed?" I ask.

"Yes. It wouldn't be right to murder an Ambassador. Even your, er, adventures can be excused as a primitive species frightened by this pesky insurgent attack," Ferrolite's cooing now, at least as much as its synthetic voice allows it. "A simple recording. We can dispense with the ceremony as the Chorus has mostly departed the Meridia. I'll even have a shuttle waiting to get you out of here as soon as we're done."

Malo's watching me. Waiting. Opinions hide behind that set face but he's playing the soldier again, waiting for his commander to say what she thinks first.

"Then tell us where to go, Ferrolite. I'll do it."

The Amigga doesn't respond with words. Instead, our chosen lift lights up, and those doors open. Waiting for us.

"It'll kill us when you're done," Malo whispers as we start to move towards the lift. "You know it's a trick."

The old me might have argued with Malo then, might have said something about how Ferrolite just gave us all the reasons why it wouldn't do that. Instead, though, I agree. "You're probably right, but what choice do we have?" I gesture at the tubes standing around us. "Do you see what they're doing here? Making more species?"

"So?"

"It doesn't matter what we do," I continue. "Whether we make it out of here or not, the Chorus will keep going until those familiars we saw on *Cobalt* or something like them supplants every other species. We might as well try to enjoy the time we have until that happens."

Malo laughs. It's a quirky, heartless, head-shaking laugh, but a laugh nonetheless. "Kaishi, what do you think we've been doing? All this time in this tower?"

"What?"

"This *is* us! Ever since I've met you, it's been one adventure after another. We've nearly died a dozen times, should have died a dozen more. We're battered, bruised, but we're still here." Malo points his finger at me. "The moment we get out of danger, you're itching to throw us right back. I see your eyes, hear your shouts when we're in the worst of it. You're a soldier, Kaishi. A fighter queen, a spear-wielding huntress of the Solare."

It's the longest speech I've ever heard Malo give. What's more, he's speaking in his own language, the words of Damantum, the

Charre. The words no Amigga can understand, a creation wholly of humans.

It gives me an idea.

"So you're saying we ought to keep this going?" I reply when Malo pauses in his parade of names. "That if we're going to walk into Ferrolite's trap, it's because that's who we are?"

"I'm saying we're fighters, Kaishi. We'll get Viera and that strange thing, T'Oli, back. Then, we'll tear this whole place down."

Now it's my turn to laugh. "Malo, you've lost it. But I think I like this new you."

"Enjoy it while it lasts."

I will, because as the lift doors shut behind us, I'm sure we won't last long.

18 / MERIDIA

Plummets of an impossible range and speed are nothing new to Sax—any given assault might require the dive-bombing insertion of the Oratus and his team in conditions ranging from adverse to apocalyptic. What he's not used to, what has his stomach feeling like a flitting feather as the lift shoots down, is the solitude. Outside of these four walls there's a mission going on; his pair is fighting for her life, for their galaxy, and Sax doesn't know when he rockets past her level on what might be Meridia's sole whole-tower lift, but he feels the separation all the same.

And devours it. Banishes it into the churn of other sensations as Aspicis' exacts a stronger pull on his descending body. From the outer edges of the atmosphere to, soon, the ground beneath the surface. The lift itself is pressurized, those doors sealing tighter as the implications of Sax's command get relayed through the lift's systems and refined into a strict set of actions meant to ensure Sax doesn't burst like an over-filled balloon as his trip commences.

Doesn't mean Sax feels nothing. Doesn't mean he's not distinctly aware of his talons resting harder on the floor, or of the vague remnants of nutrient goop searching for a way up and out his throat.

He keeps it down.

Eventually the lift settles into place and a light tone announces they've reached level zero. Sax is pretty certain he's underground. The lift begins a steamy, noisy decompression that has Sax's tiny ear holes pop as thicker air floods in through the lift's loosening doors. The decompression takes time, but this is one thing Sax doesn't want to rush: he's seen what happens when you break the pressure apart on a ship.

It's the only time he's felt pity for the Flaum crew ordered to clean up the mess.

When the doors do open, the lift barks a snappy order for Sax to leave, "There are others requesting service. Please depart."

The Chorus. Always ready to sacrifice politeness for efficiency. This time, though, Sax agrees—no reason to wait in that lift any more. Not when he can step out into a space unique from the rest of the Meridia.

None of the steel walls or austere, industrialized floors present themselves to Sax as he steps out of the lift. Level Zero starts with a cavernous entry, one that makes clear this isn't just another part of the tower. Sax sees a showcase of glittering rock formations; various blacks, deep browns, and yellows. The stones are smoothed and refined, spiking up and down from floor and ceiling, or clustered together in stacks so constructed as to make clear their origins in a planner's scheme and not natural processes. Sparkles glint out from everywhere, and at first Sax thinks the twinkles are a decorative touch, but a close inspection of a jagged mustard-yellow boulder to his right makes clear those bits are circuits. Transistors. The insides of a machine.

If confronting this strange place were to give Sax the urge to flea, the lift gives him no time to act on it. As soon as Sax's tail leaves the traveling cube's confines, its doors snap shut and the lift disappears. The sound pulls Sax's eye towards the transport and he notices there's no panel here. No way he can see to call the lift back.

Which means he's stuck. Kah, or maybe the First Chair, tricked him. Sent him down here where Sax wouldn't be able to do anything.

The realization trickles through Sax's nerves, maturing into a fine hot anger. One that he takes out on that same mustard stone. The first strike with a foreclaw tears through the yellow like fine paper, and the second, his left midclaw following in with razor points slashing, draws sparks and smoke and . . . something else.

Hot, red.

Blood?

Sax stares at the stone, at what's seeping from his slash and draining to the ground around his talons.

"Are you quite finished?" says the skittering voice of a female Flaum.

Sax turns and sees a golden—too golden to be natural—furred Flaum standing, paws clasped, in front of one of the three hollowed, arching exits from the entry chamber. Her eyes, which should be black and beady, look at Sax like flashing jade, and it takes the Oratus a moment to realize her pupils are ringed by glowing implants. That realization draws Sax into a closer inspection, and he picks out, nestled in the Flaum's fur, plenty more baubles peeking from those blonde threads.

"An ordinary Flaum? This deep in the Meridia?" the Flaum speaks again. "Even an ignorant Oratus like yourself should know better. Your species is smarter than this."

Sax doesn't know what the Flaum's talking about, so he bets on his two strengths: claws, and threats.

"I need to make sure my pair isn't trapped," Sax hisses, dripping as much menace as he can into the words. "You're going to help me, or I'll carve you up right here."

"And then what?" the Flaum replies. "You'll drink up the blood? Oratus, I allowed you to come this far, and I didn't do that so you could threaten me."

Sax tilts his head. Blinks. The Flaum *allowed* Sax?

Rather than explaining, the Flaum guesses Sax's question, turns and strides away through the earth-toned, Chorus-crafted cave. Sax takes one more look at the slashed yellow, at the visible, wounded red-brown flesh weaving between the copper and silver circuitry. Wires poke out and vanish, and the whole thing seems to pulse to the beat of some far off heart. Ideas come and go as Sax starts off after the Flaum, all coming to rest on a singular suspicion.

Following the Flaum brings Sax into a vast room, one whose base extends deeper into a machine-made basin. The same collection of rocks cluster the space, towering on top of one another and dangling down from above like bright spears. In the center, resting in a raised, golden cradle, is that suspicion.

The Amigga is massive. Easily as tall as Sax and wider still. Its skin is layered in wrinkles, and a pair of other Flaum climb over it as Sax sees the creature, each one wiping ointments or sloughing off blackened, dead parts of its flesh. Unlike other Amigga Sax has seen in this state, this one hasn't spread its tendrils all around, but looks instead to be funneling them through its massive pedestal. The rock Sax slashed back near the lifts, the pulsing piece? It all comes back here.

But to be this large? To have grown its actual body through this much space? Sax can't comprehend how old this Amigga must be. Dalachite, back on *Cobalt*, had been cycles old and still only managed a few meters of growth; thin tendrils connecting to terminals to give it control of its station. This one, this one . . .

"Old enough," the golden Flaum next to Sax says. "Numbers become meaningless when you've lived so long. Knowledge, wisdom. Those are better markers of experience."

"If you're so old, and wise, then why did you bring me here?" Sax asks. "What can an Oratus tell you that you don't already know?"

The baubles on the golden Flaum show their purpose now. Amigga are experts at twisting minds, but direct control, that takes some assistance. Dalachite learned that the hard way when Coorvin shook loose of its influence on *Cobalt*. This one here is taking no chances—the golden Flaum is as locked into the Amigga as any Sevora host would be.

"It's not what you can tell me that matters, but what you can *do* for me." The great Amigga in the center, with those pair of Flaums scrubbing it, quivers. "Like all Amigga, I am dependent on others for my own survival. A mistake we made cycles ago, when we believed what the Sevora could do would be easy to transfer. It turns out without direct control, a subject asserts its own will quite quickly." The golden Flaum keeps her claws clasped while she speaks for her master, green eyes staring at Sax. "Yet these Flaum will not outlive me. I will need assistance, eventually. Assistance I no longer think the Chorus will provide."

"You don't believe in the Chorus anymore?"

"They are a bunch of squabbling children. They've seen so little, and believe they know so much," the Amigga continues. "I, on the other hand, have witnessed the birth of real civilization. I have helped it grow through so many trials. I would not see it die because a group of Amigga believe they are better than every other thing in our galaxy."

"You want us to survive and win," Sax says.

"Yes. I want you to work with me. You will need my help, and I have much to offer. Not least, the control of the Meridia. I have already proved my side—your forces make their way up with my help, and your small strike force of humans has been able to use the lifts with my aid as well."

"Humans?" Sax doesn't understand.

"Yes. Three of them. Marauding along the upper levels. I assumed, as they seem to be enemies of the Chorus, that they belonged to your side?"

Unexpected allies, whomever they might be, ought to be used. So Sax firms up his gaze and offers an assenting nod.

"Then you will agree to our deal? You will help me survive?"

The thought of ceding any power to the Amigga makes Sax clinch his claws. They are fighting to get out of the Amiggas' control, not merely switch which one pulls the strings. Yet, it's clear Sax is going to be stuck down here if he doesn't say yes, so that's what he hisses in reply.

"I assume, because of the effort the Chorus has gone through with you, you do have the power to make this promise?" the Amigga says. "If I find out you don't, I will bring this tower down with all of you inside of it."

A threat. That's a language Sax can understand. A clear, straight line between life and endless oblivion. It's the same stance Sax would take, the same stance he's *about* to take.

"We fought against the Sevora for cycles," Sax begins. "We fought them because of what they could do to species. Take their minds, reduce them to something other than themselves. I don't really understand what you're doing to these Flaum, but if we win, you're going to release them."

The Amigga quivers again, this time violently enough to send the Flaum scampering down from the pedestal. "I cannot. They would have nothing left if I did. Their minds have been mine for so long, they would not know how to function."

"We will teach them." Sax is as surprised as anyone to find the fire in his voice. But he's been a captive long enough, he's been on the receiving end of too many tortures to let this go. The entire reason for this resistance has been to free species from the clutches of others. No exceptions. "We will do what we have to, to help them. No more control. Any species that takes care of you will do so because they wish to, either because you pay them or persuade them."

"Then perhaps I'll leave you here and strike a new deal with whomever survives," the Amigga replies. "Others will be more willing to negotiate, I'm sure."

"You said you are old, wise," Sax replies. "You said you understood how civilization works. How can you claim that, and still rob these Flaum of their souls?"

"Because from what I've seen, civilizations drive on necessity. Those who work hardest to get what they need survive and succeed. I need these Flaum, and I have taken them."

Sax opens his claws, sets them on the rocks nearby. Those yellow and black ones, juicy growths of the Amigga inside of them. "Then

I'm doing what's necessary. Help me stop the Chorus. Then you'll survive. I promise."

The Amigga's slow to respond. It keeps Sax waiting, guessing, wondering. The Oratus keeps his eyes turning, watching for blasts to the back, a sneak attack or some other deadly ambush. An Amigga's caught him off guard before, not again. Not here, not now. Sax has no time to be stunned.

"If you guarantee my survival, I can accept your terms," the Amigga says finally, breaking Sax's thought. "I will ensure the doors remain unlocked," the Amigga twitches and the Flaum next to Sax pulls out a small handheld terminal. Powers it on and it sparks to life and shows a grainy image that resolves into clarity.

"The lifts will come when called," the Amigga says and in the picture, Bas and Evva climb into the frame, loping closer to a pair of lifts with a red panel looming in front of them. The Oratus pause for a moment, glance at each other, as other fighters sneak into the frame and exchange laser fire with something off-screen.

The panel flips to green and both Bas and Evva, the pink and the red-black Oratus, stare at the sudden switch. Suspicious, as they ought to be, of any good fortune. It's only after a staccato stitch of lasers crashes into the closed lift doors to their left that Bas slaps the panel and calls the lift.

"Your friends will find the lifts take them to the safest routes. While those the Chorus uses will send them elsewhere or fail to operate at all. When the defense collapses, you will have control of the tower."

"And the Vincere?" Sax says. "Won't they just destroy the Meridia from space?"

"You would not be attempting this if you had no plan for that, I hope," the Amigga says. "If you don't, then this whole mission is folly."

So Sax mentions the Priority Beam. Shares his goal. The Amigga agrees. Provides Sax with access to the main lift all the way up. As the golden Flaum puts away the screen, showing the Oratus scrambling into their new lift, Sax does the same. Rushes back through the caves, having made a promise to a creature that should've been his greatest enemy. But he does it anyway, slipping inside the lift the Amigga calls for him.

Suction sounds as the lift pressurizes and begins its rocketing assent to the very top of the tallest tower. Towards one more chance, one more leap to save his pair, his cause, and himself.

19 / HUMAN SPIRIT

The lift descends for a long time. Far longer than any of our other rides, and down enough that I feel heavier. I suppose if you have a tower that goes all the way out of the atmosphere, the gravity might change too. Malo and I keep our metal bars in opposite hands, and keep our others held. If we're going out, we're going out together.

This level is far different from the research ones we've been exploring up till now. A large central area comes clear as soon as the doors whoosh aside, and dominating that, standing atop a dark crimson floor that bears a startling number of scratches, is a white-formed chair holding Viera. She's tied, with some sort of metal bands, around the chair. T'Oli, its two eyestalks giving the Ooblot away, is wrapped around Viera's chest, offering its hardened armor to my friend.

Surrounding Viera, from a distance, are large glass walls behind which glow plenty of terminal lights. Machines I don't recognize loom tall in the shadows, some throwing pinpoints of red light at us, at Viera, like unblinking eyes.

"Ready?" Malo asks, speaking in Charre.

"Ready." I take the lead, and feel a slight sadness as my hand slips out of his. "Viera! Are you alive?"

The Lunare's ash-haired head jerks up at my words. Her face has a bloody scratch on one cheek, and as I get further into the room, I can see she's sporting a few more wounds too; the clean silver suit she had coming off of the *Nunilite* has splotches of red all over to go with tears along the shoulders—she's been dragged. It's enough to make me angry.

That anger doesn't help me catch the mirrored Oratus waiting inside, to the right of the lift. I only get the smallest warning from Viera's eyes, from her mouth starting to form the words, and then the Oratus strikes. I try to raise the bar, but the creature ignores me and pounces on Malo instead. The warrior gets a single frantic swipe in, one that the Oratus catches with a midclaw. As the creature's tail cuts Malo's legs out from under him, the Oratus tears away Malo's weapon and throws it to the side.

I don't even get in a swing before the Oratus has its shimmering claws to Malo's throat.

"I think that's quite enough," Ferrolite announces, floating into the central room through a door in the glass. The Amigga's added a new array to its floating microjets—a pair of spindly metal arms, both of which end in what look like miners. "You understand the terms, human? Say your oath, and all of you go free. Fail to do so, and your friends pay the price."

"That wasn't the deal." It's a weak comeback, but with Malo one slip of a claw away from instant death, I'm having trouble thinking clearly. "You didn't say—"

"No, I didn't," Ferrolite cuts me off. "That's the way the galaxy works, Kaishi. You always have a second plan."

The room's frozen while Ferrolite basks in its apparent victory.

"Kaishi, don't do it," Viera says this time, and her voice carries all the pain she's in. "We're gonna die anyway. Don't give that blob the satisfaction."

"Oh, you'll say the words," Ferrolite says. "Because if you don't,

I'll make sure Earth gets razed to nothing. It'll burn. We can't have rogue species polluting the galaxy." Ferrolite pauses. "Wait, doesn't Earth have a moon? I think Kolas could use one more test of his little toy, don't you?"

I drop the bar to the floor. It clangs loud, which at least gets Ferrolite to shut up.

"You want me to talk? Show me where, because I'm guessing you're not the one that needs to hear it."

"Ignos really did a wonder with you humans. So perceptive." Ferrolite gestures with its miners towards the chair Viera's occupying, and as it does so, those metal bands looping between Viera's arms, legs, and the chair snap open. "Sit there, and look straight ahead."

Fine. I head over to Viera, reach down to help her up, when a red bolt from Ferrolite's miner hits the space between us.

"No helping. She can crawl," the Amigga says.

I throw Ferrolite a glare.

"Don't," Viera whispers through gritted teeth. "Not worth it. I can move."

Viera falls forward, putting out her arms, catching herself on her elbows as she leaves the chair. T'Oli, for its part, swirls around Viera to help her lift her arms, her knees, as my friend crawls over to the glass wall and sits back against it. Her face is drained, and those red marks are larger.

The chair's empty now, so I sit in it. Press my back against the white. I keep my arms and legs, though, out of the binders. Something Ferrolite probably notices, but the Amigga doesn't bother commenting on it. Instead, the creature floats in front and to the side of me, makes sure I can still see those bright red pinpoints of light leering down from the glass wall.

"Now, put on your best face," Ferrolite says. "This is going to go out to the entire galaxy. All of civilization will hear your oath. Are you ready?"

"Is that a question?"

"I suppose it isn't. When the little lights turn green, the words to say will project onto the glass in front of you. Repeat them exactly, or your friends will die."

My legs are loose, my palms are sweaty. I'm breathing, but it's short and shallow. This is it. This is the moment.

The lights blink green. Sharp, grass green. Like magic, wisping on the plain glass surface, white letters form up into a set of simple sentences. Five lines, and that's it. Humanity's a thrall to a species I despise, an organization I hate.

"Are you ready, Malo? Viera?" I say in Charre. "I'm not going to say the words."

"In our standard language, please," Ferrolite says to my right. "It's important we be able to understand you."

Viera, keeping her head down, mutters, "I'm with you."

"Me too," Malo echoes, his voice stretched with the claw at his throat.

T'Oli, for its part, doesn't understand what I'm saying but seems to get the gist. The Ooblot slimes off of Viera and blinks its eyes at me.

"When I say," I shout as Ferrolite continues to yell at me for talking in the wrong tongue. "I'm going to go for the Amigga. You three handle the Oratus for as long as you can. If this is being recorded, it will show we didn't give up. We fought to the end."

"Kaishi!" Ferrolite's booming its voice from all the speakers now. "Stop, or I'll have this one kill your friends anyway!"

"Just a prayer," I say to the Amigga in words it understands. "For us, on this new journey." Then I take a breath, this one full, until it feels like every inch of me is tight and ready. "Go!"

I burst off the chair towards Ferrolite, who responds with a startled shout. I don't see what happens to Malo, but given the sudden angry hissing erupting from behind me, I gather my warrior isn't dead. That's all the attention I can spare him, though, because Ferrolite's floating back and trying to get its miners angled at me. Unfortunately for the Amigga, I'm small. Fast. And I've had plenty of practice juking around trees and out of lines of bow fire.

Ferrolite's trying to get back to its glass door. I jump and one of its miner shots streaks by me, the mask keeping me safe from any harm, and I tackle the Amigga. Hit its metal arms and shove its floating body out of the doorway and back into the glass wall. Shrieks abound as Ferrolite's exoskeleton scratches the wall's surface. I'm hanging on it now, looping my left arm around Ferrolite's right side, and my hands are grabbing for the miner gripped in its holster.

The Amigga's saying things too, threats and commands and shouts, but I don't care. The miner's all that matters. But I can't get it. I'm trying, tugging and pulling and it's not coming out from its socket. Ferrolite spins, puts my back to the glass wall, and then presses me against it. The Amigga's gray-blob form is so ugly up close, and I try to look away but it's hard when the creature has me pinned. When it's crushing the air out of me.

I bring up my knees and kick out against the Amigga's spongy-soft form. Microjets might be good for floating but they're not much for resistance, and my kick gets me enough leverage to let go of Ferrolite and drop to the floor. Almost at the same time as I hit the ground, I see Malo fly across the room, red lines slicing his chest, and slam into the glass wall opposite me. Cracks form where Malo's shoulder hits, and he's slow to get up, but he's lying near my old metal bar. As Ferrolite re-orients my way, the mirrored Oratus snatches T'Oli off its back and opens its toothy maw.

"All this fighting, and you've still lost," Ferrolite says. "Instead of your loyalty, everyone is seeing your failure."

I stare at the green lights behind the Amigga. If every one of those lights is an eye through which the galaxy is seeing our last moments, then they'll see that humans won't give up.

"Yeah, well, you're ugly." I push myself away from the wall and spring at Ferrolite again. "Slide it now, Malo!" I say the words in Charre, hoping the warrior can hear me, can still act.

To the side, I see Viera make a swipe with Malo's metal bar, knocking aside the mirrored Oratus' Ooblot-clutching foreclaw. My reward for the glance is a shot to the chest, one my suit catches, and partially absorbs. Burning pain ripples from the spot, but given how close I've come to death before now, it only makes me laugh.

This time, I go below. Duck beneath Ferrolite's shooting arms and snag the metal bar as Malo slides it towards me. Ferrolite wheels itself around, expecting me to go completely underneath its bobbing body. Instead, I back up, using my feet and their grip to get behind the Amigga and line up for a hard swing. I connect, delivering as strong a stroke I can muster. The blow sends the Ferrolite careening forward into the glass wall near Malo, and the Amigga gives off a howl of purple rage to match its bruising skin.

Advantages shouldn't be lost, so I follow up the swing with a three-step approach, raising the bar above my head and planning to bring it down on what should be a final, destructive blow. Instead, just as I catch my own face reflected in the glass, the mirrored Oratus slams me with its tail, catching my stomach and flinging me, metal bar and all, back across the room. I hit the glass hard and things go hazy for a moment, with a few crystals falling around around me.

When I shake the blurs loose, I get a grim picture: the mirrored Oratus is helping Ferrolite get itself turned around. Malo's still on the ground, though he's at least sitting up. Viera's motionless over by the lift doors, and T'Oli's sliming my way, but the Ooblot's sporting a series of new dark lines on its cream-colored skin, and one of its eyes is gone entirely, the stalk waving with nothing more than a bloody stump on top.

Looks like this is it.

I get to my feet, brace against the wall to stand, the metal bar in my left hand. T'Oli gets to me and, without a word, slithers up and brings a sword to my right.

"We're not giving up!" I muster a broken shout. "You will not win!"

"No," Ferrolite responds, synthed voice tight with pain. "But neither will you."

The mirror Oratus echoes its master's words with a deep hiss. I'm ready to accept the end, and give one last look of what I hope is determination to those green lights. Let them see what I'm dying for, what I'm fighting for. We will fall, but we will fall free.

Ferrolite bids its minion to attack first, and the Oratus is happy to oblige. It reads my new weapon though, and takes a cautious approach. Its talons step near one at a time while I circle towards the center. Try to give myself enough space. Ferrolite could shoot me, but it seems content to watch as its Oratus rends me to pieces. Or maybe the collisions with the wall damaged its miners. Either way, it's me against a giant lizard.

"C'mon." I spit at the beast. "I've faced worse."

"Don't think that's true," T'Oli patters quietly.

I'm as surprised as anyone when I laugh at the words. One last joke from the Ooblot. As I wipe away a sudden set of tears, the Oratus makes its move.

Its tail comes first, snaking around my right and driving me back a step, and while I'm retreating, the Oratus cuts its strike short and jumps at me. I try to stop, try to reset my feet to stab forward, but I'm off-balance and the swing comes too slow. The Oratus clubs me with its fore- and midclaws, sending me flying back to the ground in front of the lifts. Before I can move, the Oratus jumps again, this time landing with its talons near my legs, their claws putting pressure into my ankles.

I'm trapped. I'm dead.

The Oratus hisses, looks at me and opens its jaws.

Which, for some reason, make a *whooshing* noise.

"Guess we chose the right floor after all," a second hiss, this one deeper, angrier, comes from behind me. "Get off."

The voice doesn't wait for an answer. A giant red-black Oratus flies over my face, colliding with the mirrored Oratus and driving it off of me. The red Oratus grips its enemy with all four claws and whips the creature into the weakened glass wall on the right, and the whole thing comes down in a shower of glistening shards.

I start to stand when another shape whistles by above me, green scales catching in the sparkling lights of the fallen glass. Even as the mirrored Oratus struggles up, tries to untangle itself from the mangled machines, its eyes on the red Oratus in the room's center, the new, green Oratus scales the wall behind it. I feel a gentle pressure on my shoulder and a soft hiss at my ear, "Stay down, little human."

The hiss has a verve, and as I sit back, my eyes are drawn to that green Oratus, now jumping from the wall as the mirrored enemy gets up on its talons. At the motion, a name clicks through my stunned mind, and I *know* its Lan making the dive down at the mirrored Oratus, know it's Lan wrapping her tail around my enemy's neck, pivoting and, with her momentum, flinging the mirrored Oratus out of the pile and right towards the red Oratus.

Who makes the most of the opportunity, catching and clamping down on the mirrored Oratus with her claws, holding the beast steady. Bas jumps over me, goes three long lunges, and uses a swift snap of her jaws to take care of the trapped monster. And that's it. With a clamp of those jaws, the fight is over.

Which is when I notice Ferrolite is gone.

20 / APEX

With a hiss and the clicking clank of opening locks, Sax reaches the top of the Meridia. Gravity here lessens its pull on Sax's talons, so that when he steps through the door in the Meridia's topmost chamber, Sax floats a brief moment before touching down on the black metal floor. There's no cushion, no concession made to comfort.

Instead, effort seems to have gone into looks. The floor vanishes away beneath him, a wave of shimmering dark tiles broken only in the center where, like a perfect bubble rising from a lake of tar, sits the Priority Beam. On its curved, domed surface, small nodules jab in pinks and blues. Fluorescent, short or long and always with a rounded, metallic top. They point out in all directions including back towards where Sax stands now.

What draws Sax's eyes most, though, is the view.

The top of the Meridia soars above Aspicis' atmosphere. Kissing space itself. As if in celebration of their hubris, the Chorus capped the Meridia with a clear shell. Transparent, and yet magnetized, electrified or in some other way the Sax doesn't know, it's enhanced to block the brutal cascade of harmful radiation and potential debris strikes. A faint white glows at the very edges where the glass comes into contact with the black walls surrounding Sax, which rise just over his head.

The Chorus use the view they've created, too. Dancing, luminous red bolts arc back and forth from one long antenna to another through the spacc overhead. A light show, a promise of Chorus power and resources. The display blazes and obstructs the view of the cruisers and starships assembling above the planet. Obscures the pops of fiery explosions as some of them fight each other.

It seems not every Vincere band is siding with the Chorus. Evva may even have sent a short-wave message to friends she has in the system. But that's not what Sax is here for. What he needs to do, with this beam will let him do, is tell the rest of the galaxy to come. To help them. To win.

What Sax is looking for as he goes into the room is a terminal. But there isn't one. The floor itself gives a hint of something—tiles are easy to retract and shift around, but there's no clue how.

Perhaps the Amigga down below might know. Sax casts around his eyes, looking for a camera, something that he could use to send a message to that unlikely ally. The walls of this level, though, are bare.

But, as a click and grind announces, these walls are not simple.

One of the black pieces behind Sax slides away, and then another and another until several meters worth of doors open, revealing a glaring white room opposite the lift were Sax arrived from.

Filling the new space, floating, spinning its shiny silver rings, is the First Chair. Two rings of microjets, swirling to keep the Amigga aloft, while the weapons on two others settle on Sax. Still another covered in buzzing communications devices comes to life.

"We built a bunker here for this purpose," the First Chair says in its distinct, calm monotone. "There was always a chance that the Chorus would need to call for help, and the Priority Beam makes for a good final refuge."

"Then it's serving its purpose," Sax says, turning and spreading his claws. Yet, he can't attack yet. He can't assume that he's going to figure out how to use the Priority Beam on his own.

The First Chair seems to know this too and doesn't make a move. "I don't know how you made it here. Kah and Lei vanished, and yet here you show not a scratch. That should not be possible."

"But here I am," Sax says. "Show me how to use the Priority Beam. The fight is over."

"Is it?" The First Chair says. "In spite of those few out there who choose to betray us, our forces will still win. No matter how far up the Meridia your friends get, the Vincere will still bomb it to oblivion. Nothing will be left except rubble, except your broken, shattered dreams."

"Did you forget you're still in this tower?"

"Like I said before, I don't care. I'm dead either way. The only thing that matters is making sure you and your efforts die with me."

The words are the only signal, and one Sax doesn't catch. A pair of bright red bolts lance out from the rings as the weapons spin, triggering at the precise times to send their hot death right at Sax. Who moves, but not fast enough. Nothing is faster than light.

The first bolt strikes Sax in the side, down near his waist and causes his right leg to wobble, to lose feeling. The second one hits Sax's left midclaw and shears it off at the wrist. High-powered, deadly.

There's only one way to fight an enemy that has range when you do not, and Sax closes as quickly as possible. He dives, presses with his tail, his left leg, and with what he can get from his right. It's a fumbling leap, one that falls short but nonetheless forces the First Chair to float back into its bunker.

The weapons come around again on those rings and fire off another pair of shots but now Sax is moving forward fast, digging his claws and talons in and gouging that black metal floor to propel himself along it. The shots miss. Leave smoking marks in the tiles behind Sax. The Oratus is scrambling still and now he's beneath and near the First Chair. Sax reaches up to grip with his left and right foreclaws, snagging those rings and beginning to tear when he receives a shocking reply. A heavy burst of electric energy shimmers through his metal claws and sends Sax twitching to the ground as all of his nerves lock up.

But death doesn't come.

What does come is a second sound, the clang of metal as the First Chair and its body hit the floor. The Amigga's microjets are struggling, sputtering to come back to life. For a moment both of them lay there, unable to fire, unable to attack, unable to move.

"I didn't plan for this," the First Chair's voice comes through weak, soft. The power pushing to its communications array not quite enough to give the voice its full volume. "Miners, microjets, the shock shield all at once. Congratulations, Oratus. You found a flaw in my defenses."

Sax catches the words but can't do much with them. He's trying, in the same way that he might try to move an arm or leg that's fallen asleep after lying on it all night, to restore connection, to twitch, to move to bring himself to life and when he hears the telltale whine of the jets coming back, that's when the icy hand clamps over his hearts. When he realizes he can't do it.

He can't move.

But he can roar. Long, and loud.

There's panic in the sound, there's fear and anger and loss having come so close but now with the First Chair hovering above, dangling those weapons down on him . . . it's over. One blast to the head and it's done and all Sax has fought for is ruined.

The lights die. The bunker goes dark.

In that moment of confusion Sax knows the Amigga down below can see, can help at least to some degree. Knowing he's not alone, that there's another aiding him, gives Sax the boost he needs. This is not solely his cause, but the fight for every species living in this galaxy. Every species that wants freedom and is willing to try to get it.

Just as the First Chair starts to ask what's going on, Sax pushes his tail and his left talon. He kicks himself beneath the First Chair and this time, this time, when he reaches to grab the rings there is no electric shock. There is no burst of numbing energy. Only a tremor, a taste of what might happen if Sax gives the First Chair more time.

Instead, Sax's claws dig deep. They tear the metal and rend the rings and send the First Chair rocketing away. There's a clang as the Amigga strikes the far side of the bunker, which isn't more than a few meters wide.

At the sound, lights flash back on, blinding Sax for a hot moment, then his eyes see the First Chair covered in a flow of sparks from its broken rings; one of its weapons and one of its jets show their damage in an incendiary shower.

"Unexpected," the First Chair manages to say as it cuts the power to those rings, restoring itself to a lopsided sort of hover only centimeters above the ground. "I didn't order those lights off."

"You're already losing control," Sax hisses, struggling back to his talons.

"You're running out of time to talk," the First Chair responds and swivels a second weapon towards Sax.

There's no room for fancy maneuvers, no time for bobbing and weaving. Instead, as a laser shoots into his chest, Sax charges forward and crashes into the First Chair, biting, slashing, snarling, and feeling again and again the red laser gut punch as the First Chair continues to fire.

Moments flash in fire and instinct and pain.

It's broken. There's no rings left except for the one Sax meant to leave out of his hacking, slashing, biting. The First Chair's covering itself in the dissolving acid that Amigga's use to feed, and its presence keeps Sax from carving any more into the Amigga's body.

Not that Sax needs any help to fall back. He's burned and bleeding too. Parts of himself are hollow, though any pain that's coming is being quashed now in waves of adrenaline. Stim would be nice. Any one of a number of drugs that can keep him numb. As it is, Sax's just going to have to rely on his own strength to make it through.

"Tell me," Sax says. "Tell me how to use it."

"The Priority Beam?" even in monotone, the First Chair's voice carries with it a quiver, and a weight, the dull sadness of terrible loss. "Why?"

"Because you have nothing more to lose."

Going all the way back, all the way to his first moments on Solis when he first hatched, Sax's been taught, told, ordered, that the mission comes first. Ensure the enemy's defeat, or as much of it as you can, before you die. It's an ideal that's carried Sax through countless assaults, adventures to worlds enemy and friend. Yet here he is, commanding, beseeching the very core of that vision to ignore it.

"Why?" the First Chair says. "If I've lost everything, why help the ones who took it from me?"

Sax has an answer. He knows why you might help the enemy. Why you would abandon everything you'd been taught.

"Because we're not the ones who took everything from you," Sax says. "You took it from yourselves. You lost your way, and you know it, or you wouldn't be here waiting to die. Help us clean up the galaxy. Help us make this better. That's what you want, and we're ready to give it to you."

It's not Sax's most eloquent speech. It's not going to be replayed for cycles in front of classes to study how to turn someone's mind at the last moment. But it's real, it's what he has. The First Chair, who has very little, listens.

"Then promise me," the First Chair says. "Promise me you won't destroy our species. That Amigga will have a place in your new galaxy, in your grand vision."

Another deal, another promise that Sax has no right to make and no position to guarantee. But he *can* guarantee it. As long as Sax breathes, just as he has here, the Oratus can fight to make sure the words he says are honored. So when Sax agrees to the First Chair's ask, he does so with confidence, with courage and conviction.

"Yes," Sax hisses, a rasp low and weak as the whole of the blast are starting to take their turn. The creep along his muscles and bones stabbing, burning, aching and yet, for now, he keeps enough of it away to focus. "I will. The Amigga will not die while I have claws with which to defend them."

"Then you can have your message. You can have your victory," the First Chair says. "Though I don't think the rest of the Chorus will lay down easily."

Before Sax can say anything, the First Chair rattles off a series of words that make seemingly no sense. Names of places and people in a specific order and cadence that suggests a code. When it finishes, there is a grinding beneath the floor of the Priority Beam and from around the circular dome emerges a series of terminals. The screens plug into the nubs, and as each one connects, the screens large and small light up and show in greens and reds when they've linked to quantum satellites far beyond the planet.

This is how it works, this is how the Priority Beam reaches all corners of the galaxy and moments. How it can transmit beyond the confining speed of light and send Sax's request, his plea.

Near the bunker, two more panels in the floor shift aside and raise a simple interface. An interface for typing words and that's all. Visual data can't make it so far, can't make it to the simple itemized connection of the quantum network. Sax claws his way to the terminal, he's glad of it. If the first message of liberation came from a bleeding, battered, nearly dead Oratus, Sax isn't sure many would sign up.

Instead, Sax taps the words on the display. Simple, and yet complete.

"A new government has taken the Meridia and a new galaxy has begun. Come to Aspicis if you can, and claim your freedom."

Evva may want to send something longer, and doubtless the various news agencies covering this attack will have their own interpretations out before long. But this message gets the point across. Once he finishes, Sax sits back from the terminal and stares at the wall of red and green the lights across the screen. As the message goes out, as those quantum points find their counterparts, each icon on the screen changes from red to green.

It's done then. At last.

21 / *VENGEANCE*

We're bloody, bedraggled, and barely standing.

But we *are* standing.

Bas and Lan are using their claws to dab cold, gray cream along the various cuts we've suffered while the green lights on those cameras glow on. Apparently our fight was, is, being sent all over the planet, including inside the Meridia, which is how the Oratus knew to come here in the first place. The Meridia's own lifts seemed to know too—sending the Oratus to this level without them having to choose it.

"What?" I manage to ask.

"Perhaps someone wants you to live," Bas says, turning a couple of her claws up in a question. "Sax, maybe. Or an Amigga tired of the Chorus running things."

Bas says Evva might know too, but the commander's already left, gone off to reunite with some of their other forces. Bas and Lan, though, have a few vials of the cream and they use it liberally.

"This itches. Really bad." I bite my lip to keep from scratching at the line on my left arm where, I gather, some of the broken glass must have made a cut.

"That's the nanobots," Bas hisses as she works on Viera's more numerous wounds. "You'll get used to it. They're putting you back together."

I don't even want to know what 'nanobots' are, and suppress any fear of the things getting inside of me. T'Oli sees my nervousness and tries to tell me that nanobots are why I'm still alive at all—after the seed ship, these tiny, invisible things put my body back together.

"Doesn't mean I have to like them," I say, then spare a look for Malo, whose getting the first aid treatment from Lan. He's going to have a couple of new scars across his chest, and his shoulder's looking stiff after Lan popped it back into place. "You doing all right, Malo?"

"I've lived through worse." Malo flicks a finger towards Bas. "First time I met her, it was almost as bad."

I'd forgotten about how Sax and Bas thrashed Malo and Viera around the jungle when they kidnapped me from Earth's surface. Back then I was still in thrall to the Sevora, back then I didn't know anything.

"Where is Sax?" I ask Bas.

"Somewhere in this tower," the Oratus hisses back at me. "Causing problems, as always. After you, I'm going to find him."

"Not alone," Lan adds.

"You're not going after Evva?"

Bas laughs. "I think we'll all wind up at the same place before this is over."

I would ask where that might be, but my eyes float to the lift across from me. The right one of the two, a silver color and the one Ferrolite must have taken. The one to its left is shaded red, and Bas says that means it's dedicated to the media levels of the Meridia, and I can't imagine Ferrolite docking its escape shuttle anywhere this low. The Amigga's pet Oratus might be dead—Lan insisted we leave the body in clear shot of the cameras, so that anyone watching understands this is real—but Ferrolite's continued existence has taken priority on my list of things to handle while I'm here.

Apparently, a mission to join the Chorus has turned into a violent protest against most things the Chorus stands for. Guess I'm not the best choice for Ambassador.

Bas steps away from Viera, who manages not to collapse all over again. Instead, the Lunare just looks tired, and I can empathize. Without the edge-of-death boost keeping me ready to run, my own muscles are telling me it's time to grab a nap. Malo, too, looks like he's best equipped for a solid chunk of hours on one of those red sponge beds the galaxy likes.

Which is why I ask, "Have any stim?"

Lan snaps her eyes to me, cocks her head at an angle. "Why do you want that?"

"Have an Amigga to catch." I have no idea if it's possible, but if there's any chance, any chance at all . . .

Bas appreciates my sentiments with a low hiss of her own, then she scoops another black-topped vial off of her mask with her midclaws. "I was saving this for Sax, but I think you might be able to use it more."

"Wait," Viera interrupts. "You want to go after Ferrolite? Now?" When I don't shoot down the idea, Viera's hands go up. "Why bother? Look at these two, and that other one, Evva—they're going to have this thing won in a few minutes. Then we'll have all the time to track down the Amigga, rather than right now, when we're half dead."

"That's what we thought about the Sevora," Bas says. "Many times we thought we had them gone, so we held back. Did not over-commit. And every time, they would slip away and come back stronger than we anticipated. If you can crush your foe, then crush them."

"Or eat them," Lan adds.

"Yes, eating them is good too. Especially if they are tasty," Bas hisses. "I have never eaten an Amigga, though."

Viera's throwing disgusted looks at both Oratus, and I'm trying and failing to hold back some much-needed laughter. It's a moment that dies when I catch T'Oli slithering over to Ferrolite's chosen lift, the Ooblot's sole eye stalk a clear reminder that, nanobots aside, we're not getting out of this unscathed.

"I'm with Kaishi," Malo says. "We have to stand up for our species. Ferrolite wanted credit for bringing us to the Chorus. Let's give it what it's looking for."

"If this gets us killed, I'm holding it against you both." Viera looks like she wants to add a few more gripes, but Bas's outstretched claw coated in stim interrupts, and after that buzz, Viera's objections die away in a frenzy of distracted twitching.

Which is how the three of us, with T'Oli riding on my shoulders, wind up on Ferrolite's lift heading up. I didn't expect our options to be so narrow, but it turns out the Meridia doesn't have many levels designed for docking. There's the one we came in on, near the Chorus and meant for visitors and reserved as such. Then another five set aside for Chorus members themselves and their various entourages. Beyond those, there's only one more level on the tower, labeled for emergencies or high priority visits. I'd say Ferrolite's evacuation qualifies as both, so that's where we choose to go.

"Are you going to be ok, with one eye?" I ask the Ooblot as the lift scurries up. I have to talk because the stim is hitting every nerve like lightning, and if I don't say anything, I'm afraid I'll be like Malo, who's busy clenching and opening his fists, or Viera, who seems like she's hyperventilating in the corner.

"I will have it replaced later with a mechanical version. Until then, my depth perception will be off. Please don't ask me to aim. Or judge distance."

T'Oli says 'later' like it expects to make it to some future beyond the now, and I guess I'm there too, drifting as our lift rises to what I'll do first when I get back to Earth. Maybe it's being optimistic, but, well, maybe we deserve some optimism after all this?

The lift hits its mark and the doors whoosh open into a thin entryway that goes into a lobby sporting three triple-wide doors. One for each of the emergency bays, I gather. All of them are closed, and there's no clear one Ferrolite's chosen to use.

"It went that way," Viera points at the one to our right and I'm about to ask how she knows when I realize the evidence is at our feet.

Black lines lead to the left and straight ahead to doorways, but an amber-yellow glistens towards the right. Of course they'd light up the floor—smoke and such climbs to the ceiling, and you might not have time to mess with terminals.

"Are we ready?" I ask, heading to the marked door.

Bas and Lan each gave us a miner, so Malo and Viera have some lasers ready to go. I'm holding my scavenged tool, and T'Oli's made a blade of itself again, putting us in as good a shape as we're going to get. That we're only standing because of a heavy dose of drugs is a fact I'm choosing to ignore.

When we get close, the door opens on its own accord, no panel push required, which I guess fits the idea of emergencies. On the other side is, indeed, a shuttle, though a smaller one than I've used before. At first glance, this resembles a cone, though without the strict separation of cockpit and passenger hold. It's been painted too, a deep blue with a small set of lime-green circles. Chorus colors. There's no boarding ramp that I can see. Only a small platform lowered from the craft's center. The rest of the space is lit in white, and decorations are non-existent. Racks of various things litter the sides, no doubt placed in case a last second fix is necessary to escape.

Floating in front of it, barking orders at a trio of Flaum guards, is Ferrolite. Its last command, to send the guards back our way, dies as the door opens.

I can imagine what the Flaum see as they turn our way: a trio of beaten, bloodied creatures from a new species, two holding miners and a third wielding a crude metal bar and what looks like a pearl sword with a single eye bobbing from it. Where that falls in terms of Flaum nightmares, I don't know, but it's strange enough that, instead of engaging, the three guards break from their frozen moment to dash to the shuttle's loading platform and start ascending.

"Cowards!" Ferrolite calls after them, and the Amigga starts to float their way, but its microjets, possibly damaged from our fight, putter too slow. The platform's gone up and in before the Amigga gets there. "You'll all die for betraying the Chorus!"

"Aren't you a little beyond those threats?" I say to Ferrolite as we walk forward in a line. Malo's on my right, Viera's on my left, both with miners raised. "I don't think your Chorus is going to help you now."

Ferrolite rotates back towards us, and before it turns, I get a good look at the massive purple bruise across its back. Guess my strike did some work after all.

"No," Ferrolite says, and its synthed words are low-toned, somehow melancholy in their unnatural verve. "No, it won't."

"Sounds like you're giving up," Viera cracks.

"Aren't I?" Ferrolite replies. As the Amigga speaks, the shuttle starts up a whine as its jets power to full life. "I've been abandoned by my own guards. I've failed to capture the allegiance of a new species. Even if I survive this day, I'll be nothing to the Chorus. I'll never get a place."

"If you're expecting pity . . ." I'm almost within striking distance. Malo and Viera know to shoot if there's a risk, but until then, I want the final strike. It's my job, my duty as both Empress and ambassador, or so I tell myself.

"Reality is what it is," Ferrolite says. "For me, it is the end. For you, the same is likely true. If the Meridia is likely to fall, as inconceivable as that may be, the Vincere will raze it to the ground and burn your leaders alive in the process. Then, the Chorus will build a new one. The galaxy will remain the same."

"But you won't be in it."

The shuttle begins to move, and as it does, the slate-gray wall to our left splits apart, revealing a view of space and the Vincere ships occupying it. A blue-tinged light washes over it, and I've taken off from enough space stations now to know that's the magnetic shield, keeping our air, ourselves from getting pulled out into the infinite.

I raise T'Oli, bringing its Ooblot-sword to bear. "Last words, Ferrolite."

The Amigga, with its broken exoskeleton still hanging around it, doesn't have any eyes or arms, no mouth or shoulders with which to make known its emotions. Instead, it floats, still and ugly. "Kill me then. Do what you came to do."

Not long after I first found Ignos, I stood at the top of our tribe's Tier. After all of the promises Ignos told me to make, my own people wanted me to plunge a black-glass knife into a captive. Like Ferrolite, the captive was helpless. Like Ferrolite, who floats still in front of me, weaponless and without hope, the captive had accepted his fate. The Amigga has threatened us, has tried to force me to submit humanity to the Chorus' will even after I'd changed my mind, and had done it all for personal gain.

And yet.

I couldn't perform the sacrifice then, because I was too scared. Too new to the consequences of power and the terrible decisions that must come with it. Since then, I'd played the merciless leader. I'd executed my share of sacrifices and enemies alike because I thought such things were necessary. Such things were expected.

But maybe it's time for those expectations to change.

A pop-bang sounds as the shuttle boosts out of the bay, and as it soars from the room, a bright red bolt fires from the sole cannon on the shuttle's top. Compared to the massive light-shows put on by the Vincere's larger ships, the flash here is small, targeted. It's also enough, as the laser strikes the side wall of the back, to cause the magnetic shield to flicker. Sparks fly from the hit, and suck out into space as vacuum pulls at us for a moment.

"Run!" T'Oli patters from my hand. "The shield is failing!"

The blue tinge vanishes again as T'Oli's words get my legs into motion and the pull jerks me back, towards black space. Whistling air blows my hair, pulls the breath from my mouth. Viera, nearest to the door, gets close and it jerks open. We're not trapped, yet.

"Kaishi!" Malo shouts. "Your bar!"

The warrior has it right—with the shield flickering, it's hard to take more than a step or two at a time, but Malo reaches Viera's outstretched arm and with his own right hand, grabs my left, holding the metal bar. Together, we pull against the failing shield. Closer, with every lunge, towards the door.

Over the random pops, another whine makes itself clear, and against my own judgment I look and see Ferrolite's microjets struggling against the vacuum's pressure. With nothing to hold onto, the Amigga jerks back a meter or so every time the shield dissipates, and only manages to stop its momentum during the breaks. The Amigga's going to get sucked out before too long.

"You can't save it," T'Oli patters loud, its sole eye following mine at the Amigga.

"No, but you can. Stretch, T'Oli," I say. "Prove we're not like them."

The Ooblot hesitates and Malo gets us another long step closer to the door.

"Ferrolite isn't the Sevora! The Amigga created us, and the Oratus. They can't all be evil!" I shout the words, and Ferrolite twitches towards me as it fights its slow suck into oblivion. I'm not sure my argument is all that good, but now, more than anything, I want Ferrolite to live, to understand how wrong it was. To accept, maybe, that humans aren't the mistake all the Amigga seem to think we are.

T'Oli, at last, buys into my wish. The Ooblot stretches out from my right hand, looping and hardening part of itself around my wrist and using the pull of a vacuum beat to fly like a thrown rope through the bay towards the Amigga. There, the Ooblot wraps itself around Ferrolite's broken exoskeleton.

"Pull, Malo!" I call to my warrior, and he does.

Viera's bracing herself against the door and together the four of us reel each other in one by one, with Ferrolite sneaking inside as the shield flickers and fails for what sounds like the last time. A brief alarm sounds and a harder, thicker slat slams down and covers the door we just came through, leaving us scattered around the center of the level. Safe, alive, and breathing.

"You saved me," Ferrolite's monotone fails to send any gratitude, but I assume it's there.

"Why'd they shoot the shield?" Viera shouts when she gets her breath back. "What's the point of that?"

"Disobeying an Amigga means death," Ferrolite replies, hovering just inside the door. "They likely thought killing me would spare their own lives. Now, I will enjoy taking each and every one of their souls, slowly."

"No," I stand up while T'Oli untangles itself from the two of us. "You'll do nothing except what we say. All the killing, the executions and the dominance, all that stops now."

Ferrolite doesn't say anything for a moment, until Malo, Viera and I are all standing, all facing it. "You think, because you saved me, the Chorus will strike a deal with you? I am nothing to them."

"But you could be," I say. "We're going to win this war. When it's done, the Amigga will need someone to speak for them. Someone who understands us, and who's willing to work with the Oratus."

If there's a key to this Amigga, it's ambition. It's the chance at glory, respect, and power. Now that I know how Ferrolite operates, I think I can work with it. Bas, Evva, and the others can as well.

Ferrolite, too, seems to see its path forward—it doesn't object to my offer, and with Viera keeping a miner leveled at it, the four of us return to the lift, and head higher.

22 / PAIRED

He's sent the message. Very soon, the entire galaxy is going to question its allegiances. The Vincere's going to have to choose a side. Or, more likely, engage in a war with itself.

"So many are going to die," the First Chair crackles as its voice systems, apparently damaged, work to translate the Amigga's thoughts into words.

"So many already were," Sax says. He's stepped away from the terminal back over to the First Chair's bunker, where he can keep a watch on the Amigga. "Only they didn't know it."

"How many of them will you kill?"

Sax looks at the broken creature in front of him. Those metal rings are twisted and snapped, the occasional spark bursting from a gouged microjet or a miner Sax bit in half. The First Chair, for all its position, for all its supposed power, is nothing but a blob. Entirely dependent on the systems it's built. It's almost pathetic, except Sax knows he's just as reliant on those same systems. He might be a weapon, but he doesn't know how to grow his own food, repair a starship, or colonize a world.

"As few of them as possible," Sax hisses finally. "Every death will be a failure."

The First Chair absorbs the words as Sax crouches and, wrapping his tail around his talons, sits next to the Amigga. It's more comfortable this way, and Sax's throbbing body feels better against the cool hard floor.

"We started out that way too," the First Chair says. "A noble species, and one not as helpless as you find us today. We had limbs once, bodies more suited to catching prey in our watery home."

"You couldn't have known."

"We learned how to store recordings long before we decided that knowledge was the only currency that really mattered," the First Chair says, and Sax begins to realize he's listening to a confessional for the Amigga as a whole. "You can watch Amigga from before, living lives impossible to us now. Before we changed our own genetic make-up, long after we subjugated the Flaum and pushed them into service. Once you have someone to lift a glass, fly a ship for you, why worry about it yourself?"

"Or fight a war for you."

"Exactly. We chased after the one thing no other species could, and look where it brought us."

"You ruled everything. For a long time."

"And how many subjects would say we did a good job of it?"

Sax looks at his claws, metal-made. Unnatural. His tongue brushes along the inside of his teeth, still his from birth. His eyes blink, turn towards the arcing red lightning fixed to the top of the Meridia, flashing against dark space and the popcorn explosions as Vincere ships swirl and fight one another. The message is getting through, allegiances are being forged and broken in blood.

"I would," Sax rasps. "We would not exist without your kind, and until you went too far, we served without question."

Across the room, a lift door opens wide and reveals someone Sax thought he'd never see again. Bas claws her way through the chamber with a pair of long leaps, landing next to Sax and with one of her talons pressing against the grounded First Chair.

"Leave it," Sax says. "The Amigga's already given up."

"This one tried to kill you," Bas hisses. "I have no mercy for it."

"I expect none," the First Chair replies, its voice fractured now, broken as the technology driving its speech begins to fail. "You were made to be predators. Do not betray your nature."

The word that sticks with Sax, lying wounded and exhausted, is *made*. The Oratus were designed to be one thing, but if there's anything Evva, Bas, and Sax have proved with this entire operation, it's that they are more than what they were made to be.

"Sorry," Sax says, "but Amigga taste awful."

"So I've heard," Bas echoes, and a glimmer comes to those golden eyes of hers as she catches what Sax is thinking. "We don't want to eat you."

"Mercy?" the First Chair says. "I would not have thought the Oratus capable of it."

"This isn't mercy," Sax hisses, air whistling through his burned vents. "You've used us for so long, now it's our turn."

Evva is the leader of their uprising, her black and red scales the visage that drives their forces forward, that frames their vision. The First Chair is the same for the Chorus, a leader synonymous with a government. Taking, and making, the Amigga turn against its former allies and speak out against the Amigga's endless cruelty, that is true justice, and for the First Chair, far from a merciful ending.

But in its current state, with its rings lying broken on the ground, its microjets powerless and shooting the occasional spark across the floor, and with Bas sticking a talon right up against its rippled, gray body, the Amigga has no options. No choices. Just like the First Chair intended for the Oratus.

"Time to go?" Bas says, her tail winding around and helping push Sax up until he's standing on his talons, his own tail doing what it can to keep him balanced.

"Yes."

Sax takes one more look at the Priority Beam as they head towards the lift down. It's still lit, still pushing Sax's message to the galaxy's corners. Strange to see a mission accomplished that didn't end in blood, destruction, or extinction. A feeling Sax could get used to. Some of the time, anyway.

Bas carries the First Chair—the low gravity up here makes it easy to hold the Amigga in her claws, and the Amigga doesn't bother protesting. Resigned to its fate, or accepting it. Not that it matters.

For once, the Oratus are in control.

23 / THE LAST CYCLE

This time, the lift goes where I want it to; back to where I nearly sold out my species to the First Chair. To the top of the Meridia.

We're silent during the ride. Ferrolite floats towards the back of the lift with Viera next to it, her miner ready to fire should the Amigga feel like doing anything, anything at all. T'Oli's riding my left arm, where it can monitor what the lift's doing. Malo's with me, his hand near mine but his eyes, like mine, staring ahead at the steel doors. His mind somewhere I can't place.

When we broke out of the safe room Ferrolite stashed us inside at the start of this, I had thought we'd be able to clear up the shroud around human history. I had thought that, by destroying our origins at the hands of a rogue Amigga, we'd be able to preserve some measure of dignity as a species. That maybe I wouldn't feel like a pawn. An experiment the Amigga failed to throw in the trash.

Instead we'd all nearly died. T'Oli had lost an eye. Viera, Malo and I are all hurting, and for what?

"Don't question yourself," Malo whispers as the lift climbs.

"How'd you know?"

"You close your eyes tight when you're doing that. And, you're kind of hurting my hand."

I didn't even notice that I'd grabbed it. That I'm squeezing it tight.

"I don't want to be wrong," I say, letting go.

"No way to know for sure. I didn't know if taking you from your tribe was the right move. The Emperor was the holiest person in Damantum. Someone claiming to hear from Ignos probably ought to be seen as a threat."

"What changed your mind?"

"The conviction." Malo smiles, memories dancing around his eyes. "The way you spoke on the Tier showed you believed."

"Or that I could say what Ignos told me to."

"No Sevora could do that. Ignos may have given you the words, but you spoke them."

The lift slows, settles in for its stop. This high up, the gravity's low and as the lift comes to its rest my feet bob ever so slightly off the floor.

"I still believe in us, Malo," I say as my toes touch the metal floor again. "Humans are the equals of anyone."

"See? That's what I mean. Conviction."

When the lift doors open and we leave, I'm smiling too. Small, determined, but a smile. One that vanishes as we enter the familiar ring around the Chorus chamber and see a trio in front of us. A Vyphen, looking battle-scarred and tired, a Whelk with what looks like a giant miner lancing straight out from its ruby-red body, and an ash-black Flaum that comes swirling through deep memories to my mind.

"Coorvin?" I manage to dredge up the creature's name.

Before I finish, the Whelk's trained its miner on me. With the barrel in my face the weapon's even larger than I thought it'd be at first, and now I'm getting nervous. If this thing's a member of the Chorus, it might liquidate all of us before we even start to move.

"Fire and the orb gets it," Viera preempts any answer to my question with the threat from behind me.

"Why should I care?" the Vyphen replies, the creature's eyes moving from me over my shoulder, towards Ferrolite. "That thing isn't any friend of ours."

I permit myself a half-sliver of calm. Only a half. I try looking non-threatening, spread my hands out wide, and say Coorvin's name again. This time, I follow it up with, "Want to tell your friends that we're, uh, friends?"

The Flaum tilts his head at me, and I don't see much kindness in that face. "Friends? Last time I saw your species, you were leaving Sax, Bas, and I to die as *Cobalt* fell apart."

Oh. Yeah.

"That wasn't my fault! The Sevora told me to do that."

Now the Vyphen and Whelk are glancing back and forth between Coorvin, myself, and the Amigga, their expressions saying they're sliding towards shooting us all first and figuring out if we're dangerous later. Coorvin, though, doesn't let it get that far. The Flaum sighs, places a hand on the barrel of the Whelk's miner and pushes it to the side.

"These are humans," Coorvin says.

"Worthless ones," Ferrolite grumbles, and Viera gives the creature a light smack with the butt of her miner.

"Humans?" the Vyphen asks. "Should I know what these are?"

The question gives me a chance to lay out the concise version of human history, which comes out to about three sentences: we're from a planet called Earth, the Sevora landed there and brought all kinds of awful with them, and now the Chorus found us and brought us here. I don't mention Ignos, I don't talk about how the Amigga thought we were the answer to their Sevora problem, and I definitely don't mention how the Chorus decided we were better off annihilated than allowed to survive.

"Sounds like they're on our side," the Vyphen says.

"I don't trust them," the Whelk counters.

"You don't trust anyone," Coorvin says.

"I trust you both."

"Only because I pay you." The Vyphen holds up a feathered limb to forestall another comeback and turns to me. "If you're all the way up here, holding an Amigga hostage, you must have more of a story."

"I do, and I'll tell you. Later." I nod past the trio. "Where are Bas and Lan? I need to speak to them."

What I don't say is that I want to leave this place. That I want to get back to Earth as fast as possible so that I can stand with my people when the Chorus decides to send their Oratus to wipe all of us away.

The Vyphen gets the point, thankfully, and, after sending the Whelk to give Ferrolite additional assurance of its demise should any escape be considered, we walk through one of the section tunnels to a chamber I'd hoped never to see again.

The Chorus room is back to its classic red and black. Each of the Amigga booths are empty, without the faintest sign of the dozen creatures and their attendants that cast who knows how many species to their ultimate ends. Or tried to, anyway.

Lan, and the larger Oratus they called Evva occupy the center. When she sees me, Lan breaks out into a toothy grin.

"Your hunt was successful," Lan hisses first.

"Barely," I reply. "Where's Bas?"

"Her pair needs her," Lan says, and the smallest echo of concern comes through. "I would have gone as well, but Evva must be protected. Though, it seems, not from this Amigga."

It's strange, seeing the very creatures that struck so much fear into me not all that long ago, laughing at Ferrolite. Seeing the Oratus give us a friendly greeting melts the last of the ice away from the Vyphen and Whelk as well, and conversations break out between us. I fall into a re-telling of where we went in the Meridia, and when Lan asks for the fuller story, I tell that too. Still, I keep humanity's origins a secret.

Evva stays silent as I tell my tale, I see her eyes tighten as I talk about the archives, when I lie and say we wound up there after trying to find our way down the giant tower to where the fighting was taking place. Whatever goes on inside her mind, she chooses not to confront me, and waits until I'm done to speak.

"You nearly pledged your species to the Chorus," Evva says when I'm done, her voice a stronger timber than Lan's. I recognize the weight—confidence. I'd heard it in the Emperor, in Dalachite on *Cobalt*, and even in Malo while Ignos held his body and commanded me to surrender.

"Because I did not, I think I've killed us."

"No," Evva says the word. "I don't think the Chorus will be much of a threat anymore."

"They won't give up just because you took this tower," Ferrolite calls, having drifted close enough to hear our conversation. "The Vincere will take it back. You can't hope to hold it."

"The Vincere no longer works for you," Evva says. "I would choose your next words carefully, Amigga. Your species may have a part to play in what comes, and you would seem to be in a good position to determine how big a part that is."

Ferrolite, a slave to ambition, falls silent. Which returns the Oratus gazes to me. It's not much of a guess to see what they're looking for.

"You want the same thing the Chorus do," I say to the dozens of teeth, those shimmering scales, those yellow-black eyes.

Evva doesn't deny it.

"The Amigga ruled by themselves," the Oratus says. "We will do things differently. A council, yes, but one made up of every species. Yours included."

Sit in one of those red-lit sections? Live in this tower, or on the world far below? This wouldn't be the servitude of the Chorus, but it wouldn't be home either. I throw a glance back to Malo and he meets me, steady and ready to accept whatever I choose.

"Kaishi," Viera's voice speaks up. "If you don't want it, I'll take it."

That has all of us turning towards the Lunare, who still has her miner trained on the Amigga.

"What?" Viera says. "Always said I liked seeing new places. No offense Kaishi, but if you're going back to those tunnels, or that sweaty city of yours, I'd rather stay here. Make sure the lizards don't get too power-hungry."

"Lizards?" Evva hisses.

And I laugh. I laugh because Viera's wearing a cocky smile that says she's more than up for the challenge. Equipped with an attitude that would have earned her a swift death from the Chorus, Viera might be the voice humans would need here. She'd make sure we wouldn't get thrown around, that Earth would be safe.

Or she'd annoy everyone so much the Oratus would eat her.

There's a lot of eyes staring at me. A lot of teeth, too. The red light inside the chamber, all that space suddenly seems big. Too big. I'd asked for destiny and it came for me, but I never really chose it. Here, though, my own life, Viera's, and humanity's role in the galaxy at large all comes down to a word from my lips.

"Can I take a moment?" I say, and it's softer than I mean, but I want to get away, to breathe and think without all the eyes.

Malo catches my thought and takes me by the hand, guides me out as the Oratus grant my wish with a hissing assent. I'm barely out from the middle before Evva starts up behind me on some other task, so I don't feel all that rushed.

"Thanks," I tell Malo once we're outside, back in the cold metal of the ring. "It was a lot, in there."

"Even Empresses need a break sometimes."

I nod, and start walking. Without the threat of death or under Ferrolite's demanding direction, the Chorus level seems nice. Evva's troops—I'm guessing—have commandeered the room controlling all the various screens, and the terminals have reverted to their prior cascade of pictures from across the galaxy. The foreign landscapes, covered in icy vistas, rocky plains, and sprawling purple jungles, calm me down. Distract me from my own lingering pains.

"You're worried about her?" Malo ventures the question after we've gone a quarter way around.

"I feel like this is my responsibility. I brought us this far, it's not fair for me to walk away."

"I think you've earned that right." Malo's voice doesn't sound like my father, but it's something I could imagine him saying. "I thought part of being a leader meant knowing what your people could do better than you."

"You think Viera would make a good ambassador?"

"I don't think she'd let them kill us." Malo laughs. "Or push us around."

"I'm afraid she doesn't have the patience for it."

"How do you know?"

I pause. We've reached the part of the ring where our old safe room sits to my left. The door's open, the panel green, and through it I can see the fringe of Aspicis' blue atmosphere. Malo's question is a good one. I've been on the run with Viera, in plenty of danger, but the time we spent running Damantum before the Oratus arrived was brief. It's hard to pay attention to a friend when you're learning everything on the fly.

"Viera did manage to live with our tribe for a while," I say slow, feeling out the idea. "She didn't manage to offend us too much."

"Compare that with you," Malo says. "Everywhere you go either falls apart or gets attacked."

"Hey."

Malo laughs and I can't hate that.

We make it back to the red-lit center ring and I ask Viera one last time if she's willing to accept the job. Her response is a little too enthusiastic, and prompts a sigh from Ferrolite, one which Viera rewards with another swat of her miner.

"You can't do that to everyone you don't like, you know," I say as Ferrolite floats away from her. "You have to talk to them."

"Don't think the new government's started yet," Viera replies. "When it does, I'll be nice. Nice enough, anyway."

Even as I roll my eyes, my thoughts are turning to one place. The only one that really matters.

Home.

24 / A DYING STAR

For once, Sax isn't thinking about prey and predators. His claws aren't raised and his teeth aren't ready to sink into an enemy. He's not wearing a mask, nor wielding miners.

Relaxed.

The word makes him laugh, a delighted hiss and gets a glance from Bas, standing next to him in front of the many meters-high shield giving view to the purple-red expanding light show in front of them. Behind and around the two Oratus, plenty of other species are doing the same thing; watching nature's grandest spectacle while robots bring food, beverages, and all manner of other pleasures to their sides.

Above and around Sax, a sound-dampening field serves to quiet every word not coming from his pair's mouth, ensuring a magical, private experience. The old Sax would have found the inability to hear what's going on around him stressful—too easy to sneak up on someone when they can't hear you coming. The new Sax? The new Sax doesn't care.

"I don't think I've ever heard you laugh like that," Bas says, and there's concern in her eyes. "Are you all right?"

"Look around us," Sax says, and he gestures to his right, where

Plake and Agra-Red sit at the next circular pad. Beyond them, Nobaa and Engee occupy their own, and the various Flaum, Coorvin included, sit beyond Bas. "How could I not?"

Once they'd managed to square things away on Aspicis, Evva insisted the lot of them needed to go and leave her alone to work things out as various ambassadors, merchants, and power brokers flew in to stake their claim within the new galaxy. Sax wanted no part of the politics, and neither did the rest of Plake's mercenary crew.

"You're changing," Bas says. "I like it."

"I'll always be a hunter," Sax replies. "But this isn't so bad either."

A robot floating on microjets enters their sound-proof dome and slides over, using some precise magnets, a series of bowls full of strange-looking puddings, noodles, and slabs of red-brown meat, all grown right in *Nova*'s own gardens and labs.

"Do you know the last time I had a meal that wasn't nutrient goop?" Bas says as she hooks one of the slabs with her right foreclaw.

"You didn't eat a single Flaum when you took the Meridia?"

"A little bit of fur doesn't count," Bas laughs, tosses the steak into her mouth. "The last time was here, Sax."

Sax blinks. Guess that's true for him too. So much time grinding through nutrient goop-fueled jobs for the Vincere and eventually he'd stopped remembering the meals. Now he follows his pair's lead, nabs a slab of slight-singed meat, eats it. Juicy, soft, real. Sax devours a few more while Bas starts recounting how they met, and Sax realizes they'll have all the time now for the past, for each other.

The idea doesn't scare him like it would have not long ago—his pair is his purpose, and Sax has yet to fail a mission.

In front of them, deeply nestled in the blooming red, a tiny purple blossoms. Just a speck, gas expanding out into the wide infinite. Something new in a stellar cloud older than all the cycles the Chorus ever saw.

25 / WHAT'S OLD IS NEW

Damantum isn't as I left it. There's a lot more metal here, for one, and the sky isn't a clear blue because it's crowded with so many ships.

I'm standing on the Vaos, that golden temple in the middle of my city and one of the few structures left intact after the Sevora started their war. I wasn't here when it happened, but I've heard from my own people that dark shapes appeared overhead, followed by bright lances of burning energy that crashed through homes, walls, and palaces alike. The Charre, my adopted people, fled the city in all directions and plenty haven't returned in the time since, with the Vincere's help, we drove the Sevora away.

"You're frowning," Malo says. He's next to me, watching my face as the wind blows my hair into my eyes. "What's wrong?"

"Nothing. Just thinking about what happened, and what's next."

The future's everywhere in front of us, down the Vaos' many steps and stretching over a city under construction. Some of the repairs look familiar, but most are strange, with mobs of humans watching as Flaum and other species demonstrate the technologies being brought in all those ships. Viera sent notice that we'd be getting a surprise not long after Malo and I, courtesy of Plake and her shiny new Vincere ship—apparently it had belonged to a Chorus Amigga—made it home. After dropping with us, T'Oli had scurried off with a band of welcoming traders and left in search of Vee, noting that it was probably a bad idea to let a rogue Oratus wander free for too long.

While Evva and the new leadership of the Vincere sorted their thing out, plenty of planets and groups wanted to get in on what was now a wide open galaxy. Resources and expansion were the new thing, and Earth had plenty of the former, with possibilities for the latter. As such I'd already been invited to a dozen dinners aboard various cruisers, and had all sorts of strange bribes offered to me.

I'd turned them all down.

"You think all this generosity will melt your heart?" Malo says. "They're really trying."

Another wave came in the form of donations, of personnel coming with tools and trades to teach my people, and the Solare and Lunare in the jungles and mountains, about all the ways their own lives could be easier. I wasn't asked about any of these, but with our military still in shambles and my own appetite for a fight long gone, I'm not objecting to a little bit of charity.

"It's going to take them a long time." I put my hand on the altar next to me. There's still red there, a stain from a lifestyle dying away, but no more sacrifices. I encouraged the priests to worship Ignos, but without the bloodshed. Unity, cooperation. We'd give those a try and see how our god treated us. "And I don't mind. If everyone's busy with the visitors, then they're not asking me questions."

Malo laughs, shakes his head, and we watch Ignos tilt its way towards the horizon.

"I wonder how long this will last," Malo says after a minute.

"How long?"

"Everything's already changing, Kaishi. It won't be too long before the Charre decide they don't need an Empress, or warriors. We'll be part of all . . . this."

The wind picks up at the top of the temple and I relish the breeze. Too long breathing in artificial air, with the drone of a fan behind every gust. Now I get spices, the smell of baking bread and, yes, a bit of that tongue-tingling current of burning electricity.

"After all we've been through, you're worried about a little change?"

Malo looks at me, the corner of his mouth lifting up. "I suppose that sounds stupid, doesn't it? It's just that we've only made it home, and now we're losing it again."

"It's changing Malo, but it's still here." I take a step down from the top. "Come on, I can smell those peppers cooking."

AN EXCERPT FROM DROP ZONE

SEVER SQUAD BOOK ONE

He called her the wrong name. Twice. So Aurora whipped her hand back, and sent it crashing against the lunkhead's face. Skin rippled, like an earthquake, from where the heel of her palm bit into his cheek. His eyes flew up and his mouth screwed into jagged line, as though all of the nerves in his head couldn't quite comprehend what had just happened. Then he dropped to the ground. Hit the floor like a bomb. One that sent the rest of the mess into deafening quiet.

"My name's Aurora. Get it right." She said, even though the man, from his glassed gaze, definitely wouldn't remember this.

Aurora cast the same threat around the hall. Bunch of rookies. New recruits to DefenseCorp. All of them staring back at her like she was a Gnarler, all tentacles and teeth. They were scared. As well they should be.

Aurora looked at them, elbows on the steel tables. Trays full of nutrient soup. The rookies were all shades, all types. Even a few E.T.'s in the mix. A trio of willowy Casparians, their thin membranes making them almost translucent.

DefenseCorp must be expanding its horizons. Marketing to species that don't breed like rabbits, like humans. Convincing them that hard-earned cash and a big cannon were worth risking your life. Not the worst message.

It'd worked on her, after all.

"You see what happened to this guy here?" Aurora announced to the silence. "He didn't respect his superior. He didn't respect me. And when you don't respect me, you don't respect who you work for. And if you don't respect DefenseCorp, this is what happens." She pointed the body in the ground.

Another reason she liked working for DefenseCorp? This guy decorating the floor right here. None of that standard issue government regulation. Just good old-fashioned survival of the fittest. Fatter paychecks too.

Aurora resumed walking. Left the hall and the food that she didn't want behind. As fun as it was to strike some fear into the rookies, she'd only been going through the mess on her way to someplace more important: the bridge.

The Odin-class cruiser *Nautilus*. The home of nearly 200,000 people. Made from the core of an asteroid, hollowed out, refined and sent off on journeys to the most dangerous, most profitable parts of the galaxy DefenseCorp could find. Anywhere chaos planted its seeds, DefenseCorp showed up, ready to kill and clear, for the right price. The company most of the galaxy paid to handle blood work, and to clean up the aftermath.

Aurora glanced at her wristlet as she walked—an easy motion, as it was bolted to her left wrist. Embedded, if you wanted to call it that. That way they couldn't be lost. That way the batteries, if necessary, could recharge off of her own body heat. Aurora kept it running in low power mode no matter how long she was out. Until she died, anyway.

The wristlet blinked an orange alert at her. As it had been the last ten minutes. The length of time it'd taken Aurora to go from her quarters, through the mess hall, knock out the lunkhead, and now to get here.

The *Nautilus*'s bridge_was larger than most stadiums. A huge amount of space, for a huge amount of officers. Scanners, computers, giant domes for people to sit in that would provide, in case of some sort of battle, 3-D modeling of everything going on. Right now, though, the *Nautilus* was in transit. Which meant the view out the ship's front was all black, starry sparkles washed out by the blue-white interior lights. Off on the right, a pinkish nebula glowed. Pretty, if you had the time for that sort of thing.

"Took you long enough," Commander Deepak said. The man stood tall. Rippling in his skin suit that he never took off. That all DefenseCorp commanders had to wear as part of their rank. Seeing it made Aurora's standard-issue cloth itch.

A skin suit provided the usual comforts. Regulated Deepak's body temp, killed poisons that made their way into his bloodstream, and happened to look just like a snazzy crimson uniform. The collar brushed up to the bottom of Deepak's chin, a dark one covered with not a micrometer of hair.

"I tried to run, but someone got in my way." Aurora didn't bother shrugging. Deepak knew any obstacle had been removed.

"It's fine," Deepak said. "I called you because twenty minutes ago we received a covert SOS. VIP customer, so it's need to know. Your squad is being pulled from our main assignment to handle this one, and we're almost to the drop point. You have your squad ready?"

"I read the message," Aurora said. "Sever will be set to launch on time."

"And you?" Deepak replied. "You're good on the particulars?"

"It's a standard for Sever, right?" Aurora said. "Get in, raise all manner of bloody hell, then get out?"

"With the client, yes," Deepak smiled. "One warning though—you won't be getting an extraction. We can't delay our primary contract."

No extract? That didn't sound right. On occasion, Sever would do a drop and run. But that just meant the extraction would be delayed. Sever squad would hold their own, wait undercover after completing the mission and eventually some shuttle or another would show up and give them a ride back home. Deepak wasn't talking about that though. She could tell in his voice, which held a final note to it.

"What you mean?" Aurora almost added *sir*, but this wasn't the military. You didn't have to call your commanding officers titles. They weren't even really officers. Just bosses.

"It means you have to find your own way off world," Deepak said. "This contract is strictly classified. We can't have evidence that DefenseCorp was involved."

"Won't it be pretty evident? My squad doesn't operate in the dark."

"You the best, Aurora. That's why you're getting this assignment. You and Sever will figure it out. Buy a shuttle, or steal one. You'll be reimbursed."

And if they couldn't?

Aurora didn't ask the question, because she knew the answer.

Start a new sci-fi action adventure with Drop Zone, available now!

ACKNOWLEDGMENTS

The Last Cycle closes the longest series I've ever written, consisting of six novels and a pair of novellas. It's easy to say that these stories are the product of an over-active imagination and that the only requirement to telling them was to sit in front of a keyboard and type.

I wrote this series in multiple countries, on beaches and on mountainsides. In planes and in bars, restaurants, cafes and in the corners of libraries. All of those moments came with the help of others, from my wife and her endless patience with my escapes to other worlds, to the baristas whipping up espresso or the attendant carefully handing me water across full seats in turbulence so as not to spill on my computer.

In short, a series like this takes time and effort, not just by the writer, but by those who help give that writer the time and space to, well, write. So, thank you, because without your help, I never would have met Kaishi, nor traveled the stars with Sax and the Sevora.

ABOUT THE AUTHOR

A.R. Knight spins stories in a frosty house in Madison, WI, primarily owned by a pair of cats. After getting sucked into the working grind in the economic crash of the 2008, he found himself spending boring meetings soaring through space and going on grand adventures.

Eventually, spending time with podcasting, screenplays, short stories and other novels, he found a story he could fall into and a cast of characters both entertaining and full of heart.

A.R. Knight plans on jumping through to other worlds and finding new stories to tell in the limitless borders of our imagination.

Thanks, as always, for reading!

For more information:
www.adamrknight.com

To Blanche and Don

ISBNs:
Ebook: 978-1-946554-32-1
Paperback: 978-1-946554-56-7
Hardcover: 979-8-88858-086-8
Large Print: 979-8-88858-087-5
Published by Black Key Books

This is a work of fiction. Any similarity between the characters and situations within its pages and places or persons, living or dead, is unintentional and co-incidental.

www.blackkeybooks.com

www.ingramcontent.com/pod-product-compliance
Lightning Source LLC
Chambersburg PA
CBHW030617310726
48979CB00003B/765

* 9 7 9 8 8 8 8 5 8 0 8 6 8 *